Pen Pals

A Novella

by Avery Goode

Pen Pals
© 2020 by Avery Goode
Goode Gyrlz Publications, LLC
P.O. Box 311822 Atlanta, GA 31131

ISBN 13: 978-1-953230-08-9

Special Thanks and Acknowledgments

There is no me without you, Jesus. Thank you for always blessing me with Goode ideas. This next level journey that I am about to embark upon was designed purposefully by You and I am equipped for it.

To ALL my family and friends, thank you for adding your two cents here and there, rocking with me and supporting me throughout the years. It is about to be greater guys. Are you ready?

Thank you to all the readers who continue to show love to me and my books. You all make writing fun and meaningful. Much love to each of you and I hope you all are ready for the new, hot work I have coming your way.

Lastly, a special thanks to Susan Fox, the beautiful and intelligent L.O.W., and Navi Robins who delivers great graphics time and again.

All of you have added value to me as a woman and an author. I appreciate you more than words can say, but I will show you by continually delivering Goode books that you all remember years after you have read them. I love you all. Be Goode or be Goode at it! Keep up with me via Facebook: Avery Good, Instagram and Twitter @thegoodescribe, Snapchat -Shegoode or www.averygoodesworld.com.

Avery

More Goode Books by Avery Goode

Dishonest
Pillow Princess Part 1
Pillow Princess Part 2
Crying Meadows
Head Doctor
Private Practice: Head Doctor 2; A Freakquel
Meal Tickets
You, Me, and She

Coming Soon:

The Halfway House

Chapter 1

imping ain't easy, but someone had to do it. It may as well be her. But Lyric Carter did not consider herself a pimp or a madam. No, she was just a savvy businesswoman capitalizing off the world's oldest profession. The pint-sized panderer rolled over in her luxurious king-sized bed, grinning. Her business manager told her that profits were up. That was music to her ears.

"What are you smiling about?" Her boyfriend, Roman, asked.

"Something David said."

"Fuck," he said, easing down her naked body. Skillfully, he licked at the folds of her nether lips before parting them. Applying just enough pressure to stimulate her, he sucked on her clit until it hardened and became sensitive.

"Ooh, that's it baby." Her legs spread wider, allowing him better access. Tiny pulses of electricity began at the tips of her toes and traveled up her inner thighs until they reached her hot center. She pressed her ass into the mattress when a feeling of euphoria began to overtake her.

His lady was on the verge of an orgasm, so he stopped sucking, climbed on top, and hurriedly entered her. With long purposeful strokes, he brought her to the point of no return. One final, deep jab and he erupted inside her as she coated his hard dick with her juices.

"What was that all about?" She asked once her breathing returned to normal.

"I had to do something. When the first smile on my woman's face in the morning is brought on by a sixty-year-old white man, it's time to act."

She swatted his arm playfully. "Shit, David's fine ass looks like he could be Sean Connery's brother. Trust me, he could get it." Laughing out loud, she continued. "You know I'm just kidding. I was simply thinking about the quarterly report."

"It must be damned good to have you cheesing like that."

She shrugged, "it's good."

"How good is good?"

"We're in the black."

Although Roman was her man and her attorney, her business was her business. Pleasure Palate doubled as a gourmet catering and escort service. Her high-profile clientele commanded confidentiality. The women would cook a delicious main-course meal, but they were the dessert.

"I hate when you do that shit," he said angrily, rolling onto his back, glaring at the ceiling.

"Do what?"

"Lie and keep shit from me. I'm your attorney and your man."

"First of all, stop cussing at me. Second-of-all, I told you what he said. I'm not going to give you a play-by-play of every single thing we talked about if that is what you are looking for."

"Nah, I ain't buying. It is more than that. You do not smile that big over nothing. What gives?"

"Well if you must know, David said I reminded him a lot of my daddy."

"Hmph," he grunted. "I guess."

Lyric knew that her man had a problem with her father. Travis "Techwood" Carter was one of Atlanta's most notorious criminals before he was murdered. He ran the streets of the real A-T-L. From Stewart Avenue to Bankhead and everything in between, his territory was vast. If a person saw a prostitute on Stewart Avenue, she worked for Lyric's dad. Any dope that was pushed on the street was from one of his store houses. Bankhead Courts, Bowen Homes and Techwood Projects, belonged to him. He had those apartments sewed up tighter than Nino Brown did the Carter, in the movie, *New Jack City*. Even post-mortem he was a force to be reckoned with.

Roman supported everything she did. But this particular business was a point of contention with them and was the basis of many arguments.

"Pleasure Palate is cool. But I don't want my woman dealing in prostitution."

"You act like I'm selling my ass when you know I'm not. I simply coordinate the catering service and dates."

"Then that makes you a pimp, doesn't it? Just like your damned, no good father. Do you want to end up like him?"

It was a never-ending dispute that did not end well. Lyric loved Roman and did not like arguing with him. Especially over business.

"Listen, babe. There is nothing more that David said. You're my attorney, why wouldn't I share things with you?"

Doubtful, Roman sat up on the edge of the bed, with his back to her. Exhaling, Lyric got on her knees and rubbed his back.

"I love you. Let us not do this. Not today of all days." She did not tell him what day it was exactly but hoped that he remembered.

"Yeah, I guess you're right. It is Friday. I have a big meeting ahead of me today. I need my mind clear for that."

"Is that all?" She said, tilting her head to the side.

"What else could there be?" He laughed.

Out of the corner of his eye, he saw her face. Her forehead wrinkled, and her nose turned up slightly.

"Are you serious?"

He ignored her and grabbed his cellphone from the nightstand. She sat back on her feet, watching impatiently as he typed on the keypad.

"You know what?" She began irately. Before she could finish, a familiar, sexy tune began to play, and he started to sing.

"Do you know what today is? It's our anniversary."

Happily, she pulled on his shoulders, forcing him on his back before straddling him. "You remembered?" She said, planting kisses all over his face and neck.

"How could I forget. It has been four wonderful years since you and I began dating. Since the day you changed my life. But today, I'm going to change yours."

He reached under his pillow and pulled out a little black box.

"Lyric Elaine Carter, I want to have anniversaries with you for the rest of my life as your husband. Will you do me the honor of being my wife?"

Through tears of joy, she said "Yes."

Roman rolled her over and showed her how happy he was. After a couple of go-rounds in bed, the two prepared for the day ahead and went their separate ways, planning to meet-up later.

Atlanta traffic was ugly as usual but today, it did not bother Lyric. She sat on Peachtree Street headed to her office, unaffected by the gridlock some inconsiderate drivers created. What normally would take her twenty-minutes ended up taking her forty. By the time she got in her office, Alexis, her best friend, and office manager, had already given the women their appointments.

"Glad you finally decided to join us," the woman said with a bit of edge in her voice. It did not go unnoticed by Lyric, but she blew it off. Nothing was going to get under her skin today.

"Benefits of being the boss, Lexi. I come and go as I damned well please."

The woman walked over to her desk, rolling her eyes when her back was turned.

"You're in a good mood. What's up?" She picked up her cup of cappuccino and took a big swig.

"Roman asked me to marry him."

Lexi spit her coffee out. "He did what?"

"Damn. Why you say it like that? I thought you'd be happy for your girl."

"I am," she said, recovering quickly. "Just shocked. I didn't know you guys were that serious."

"We have been together four years. It does not get more serious than that. Today is our anniversary and he surprised me with this."

She held up her hand, proudly displaying the four carat, French-set, halo diamond stone on a fourteen-carat white gold band. The impressive piece of jewelry retailed for more than twenty-thousand-dollars. Because her father was into precious stones, Lexi immediately recognized the value.

"Congratulations, Sis," she said. The smile plastered on her face was as fake as the silk flowers Lyric kept around the office.

"Thanks, girl."

Lyrics office phone rang, and she walked off to tend to it, leaving her friend to stew. Pissed off, Lexi picked up her cellphone and dialed rapidly. Breathing heavy, she tapped her foot waiting for the call to connect. She had a few choice words for the person on the other end.

"Hello," she began when the phone stopped ringing.

"You have reached, four-zero-four," the recording said. She hit the end button.

She swiped to the text messaging feature and typed a quick 'we need to talk' and hit send. Not waiting for a response, she dialed another number.

"Hey it's me. Are you ready to move? This bitch is getting on my last nerve and dumb ass just proposed to her. It's time to wrap this up."

"Soon. I'm just waiting on some papers to get signed."

"Cool. I have something else that I believe will help seal the deal. I'll bring it by first thing Monday morning."

She hung up the phone just as Lyric walked back into the main office. This was her oldest friend. One whom she once loved dearly, but since Pleasure Palate took off, things changed. Lexi felt she did all the work but received very little recognition. The catering and escort service did belong to her friend, but Alexis felt like she should have been a partner instead of an employee. After all, it was her idea and she is the one who handled the day-to-day operations. Shortly, Lyric would be out of the way and Lexi would have everything her friend once had and more. Everything.

Chapter 2

alentine's Day was in less than two weeks and Pleasure Palate was slammed with special requests. Not only that, All-Star Weekend was kicking off the day after in New York City and Lyric needed adequate staff and accommodations for the extra business. She was in line to make over a million dollars in the month of February. Business was booming. Thankfully, Lyric worked well under pressure and thrived off the fast pace the lover's holiday created. She was more attentive during that time. As she was reviewing a file, she noticed that one of the girl's I-9 documentation papers were missing.

"Hmm, that's odd. Where could they be?" She went to check the files in Lexi's office.

Walking through Pleasure Palate, one would never think that it was anything other than an upscale catering company. Pictures of top chef's draped the walls, cookbooks lined the bookshelves, food magazines sat on the tables and it had a state-of-the-art kitchen that would impress Gordon Ramsey. There was also a special 'dessert' menu that her clients could choose from. Although it did have legitimate names of confections, they were actually codes for a sexual service or a particular girl the client wanted to service him or her.

For instance, a checkerboard cake was a request for a white and black girl together. A cake pop with cream was a request for a woman who gave head and swallowed. An Oreo cream pie was a request for a bi-racial woman who allowed clients to cum on her face and pie ala mode was a request for a lesbian who liked to give and receive oral sex.

On her way to her friend's office, Lyric stopped and stared at a picture of both their dad's, back in their hay day, looking like the true OG's they were. Alexis's father was the right-hand man to Lyric's dad. They were best friends. And now, their daughters were also. No one imagined that the girls would follow in their father's footsteps, but they did. Instead of the old school, ten-toes-to-the-curb-pimping that they grew up around, Lyric wanted a high-class escort service. Because Lexi was into food, it was her idea to implement the catering service. Their combined ideas and Lyrics money helped create a great business model that profited annually.

Alexis was on the phone having a heated conversation. Lyric was about to knock but nosiness got the best of her.

"I bet you she wouldn't if she knew that the same mouth you kiss her with is the same one that eats this pussy daily," Lexi said angrily.

Damn, is her man cheating on her? Lyric thought. *It could not be me.*

"What the fuck do you have to say to me that will make me change my mind?" She heard her friend say.

That's right. Let him have it, best friend. Do not take shit off these cheating ass mofo's.

Lyric was hyped up listening to the conversation. She just knew her bestie was about to lay into the dude but what she heard next was unfathomable.

"No, baby. Please, do not. I am sorry. But I just do not understand why you would do that, even after I told you that I...," she paused. "Yeah, I know. I love you, too. You're doing what you have to do now, so we can be where we want to be later."

What the fuck? Begging was the last thing she expected to hear. Her friend always appeared strong and confident. Clearly that was all an act.

"Dude must have some good dick because she's cuckoo for coco puffs," she whispered. "Knock, knock," she announced before walking in.

Lexi wiped the tears from the corners of her eyes and quickly composed herself after ending the call.

"What's up, Chica?" She asked as if nothing were wrong.

"The I-9 documents are missing from Amber's file. Do you have them here?" Lyric did not mean to sound agitated, but she was. Hearing her friend grovel to a man who was clearly seeing someone else pissed her off.

"Why are you mad at me? I do not have the papers. After I verified everything, I gave the forms to you. That is how you wanted it, remember boss?" The last word dripped sarcasm.

"That I am," Lyric retaliated. "I have searched my office high and low and the forms aren't there."

Alexis got up from her desk and walked to the file cabinet. Her heart rate increased a tad bit, but she calmed down. Now was not the time for a confrontation. She looked through each of the files of the women whose last names were Williams but did not find the file.

"It's not here. I have checked every file in the W's, and it is not here. Why are you looking for it?"

Frustrated, Lyric sat down in the chair by Lexi's desk. "All-Star Weekend's coming up. I want to send Amber but need to verify her age. She looks a lot younger than twenty-five."

"I did. Don't you trust me to do my job? Damn."

"Yep, but I need to look at her documents. Verify validity. Something about her doesn't feel right."

"Hmph, if you don't believe she can handle New York, give her something local to prove herself. Amber is an excellent cook and sexy as hell. Plus, you know that black don't crack."

A gnawing feeling ate at her insides, but Lyric agreed. "I guess you're right. Hell, we still look the same as we did in high school. We can send her out with the new client and see how she measures up."

Smiling, Lexi said, "just leave all the details to me."

After Lyric left the office for the day, Lexi called Amber and asked her to come in to see her.

"Thanks' for coming on such short notice. May I offer you anything?"

"I'm cool. What's up?"

"It's time to do work. You feel me?"

"Absolutely."

"We have a new client with deep pockets. He wants dinner and dessert tonight."

"I'm with it. Give me the details."

A few hours later, Amber was leaning over the stove, wearing nothing more than an apron and lace boy shorts. Her client, sat at the table, waiting for his meal. Dressed in dark slacks and a white, crisp dress shirt that was unbuttoned, exposing his muscular chest, he looked every bit the main course. The chicken pasta primavera was not the only thing that simmered in the kitchen. Looking at him, made her want to jump his bones.

"Dinner smells delicious. Would you be offended if I wanted dessert first though?"

"Not at all," She said. "What would you like?"

"A chocolate éclair with sweet cream sauce." He wanted to fuck her in her ass and cum in it.

Smiling, Amber walked over to him, pulled her boy shorts down and leaned over. The client stood up and unfastened his belt. His member sprang out like a Jack-in-the-box. Gently, he eased the head of his hard dick inside her tight asshole. She wiggled in delight.

"Mmm, baby I need to be paid before you go any further," she said greedily.

"I thought you'd never ask," he said, ramming his dick in all the way. "Amber Williams, you are under arrest for prostitution."

Next door, Alexis and her man sat, listening to the audio of what was going on, thanks to a bug they planted in Amber's apron.

"Got'em," the man said. "You did well, babe. Come here."

Alexis walked over to him and straddled his lap. Whenever he was happy, his dick got hard. She pulled it through his unzipped pants and sat on it.

"Ooh, la la. I love riding your dick, baby," she said, bouncing up and down on it. "Fuck this pussy, Roman. I love you."

"I love you, too," he said, kissing her hard on the mouth.

He grabbed her by the waist and pulled her into his thrusts, filling her up with all of him. As she was about to burst, the papers she was holding, slid from her fingers onto the floor. They were the I-9 forms that Lyric was looking for earlier. The copy of a birth certificate landed face up. When the juices began to pour from her body and saturate her lover's dick, she looked down and smiled. Amber was born in ninety-nine and was only sixteen years old.

Chapter 3

utterflies fluttered in Lyrics stomach. Something was off about her morning and she could not put her finger on it. Maybe it was strange because she did not wake up with Roman lying next to her. He left the night before headed to Miami, with his friends. Whatever was going on inside, grabbed a hold and would not let go.

"What's going on the reason you're feeling like this, lady?" She asked herself out loud.

Shaking her head to clear it of negative thoughts, she prepared for the day ahead. There were several things on her agenda that needed to be handled. Flight arrangements needed to be made. Housing accommodations had to be confirmed and decisions on which girls would be lucky enough to go to New York had to be finalized.

Amber would not be taking the trip to the Big Apple as punishment for missing an assignment. Alexis told her that the young girl called off sick at the last minute. Another lady stepped up in the nick of time to cook for him and his guests at the dinner party he hosted. The catering-escort service had a reputation built on quality and professionalism. This was supposed to be a food-only assignment. Not all their clients ordered from the dessert menu.

Once she was in the car, Lyric called Roman. It went straight to voice mail. She dialed Lexi's phone. Same thing.

"Well, damn," she said. "I'll just see her in the office."

It did not take her long to navigate through the mid-morning traffic. When she pulled up in front of her office there were a few cars there, but Alexis's was not one of them. She reached in the back seat, grabbed her bag, and headed inside. The receptionist and three of her ladies were there.

"Hey," Bella, a beautiful Afro-Asian woman said.

"Hey, ladybug," she replied. "Have you heard from Lexi?"

"Yes, ma'am. She said she would be in after an appointment."

"Hmm, okay."

Shaking her head, she headed towards her office. Once inside, she closed the door behind her, sat at the desk and put her head down. For reasons unknown, tears welled in her eyes. She had not felt like this since her dad died. Frustrated, she let the tears fall, realizing that today was her father's birthday, and it was him that she was missing all along. A commotion in the outer office got her attention. Just as she stood, her office door swung open.

"Lyric Elaine Carter, you are under arrest for felony pandering, pimping under-aged participants and human trafficking."

"What the fuck! This is ridiculous. Bella, call Roman and David and tell them what is going on. Now!" She yelled as the man was placing her in handcuffs. The receptionist could not make the phone call. She, along with the other women, were also in cuffs. The office was swarming with Georgia Bureau of Investigations agents and Atlanta police officers. Stunned, Lyric looked on as they ransacked her office.

Every computer was unplugged and placed in large, clear plastic bags. All the files were placed in bankers' boxes and marked. Each menu was collected, bagged, and tagged. Even the food in her storage warehouse and freezers were checked. A photographer took pictures of her office and each item that was confiscated, was now considered evidence.

"You have the right to remain silent," the detective said. "Anything you say can and will be used against you in a court of law. You have the right to an attorney. If you cannot afford an attorney, one will be provided for you. Do you understand the rights I have just read to you?"

"Yep," she mumbled.

"With these rights in mind, do you wish to speak to me?"

"Nope, but I would like to call my attorney before we leave so he can meet me. Where are you taking me?"

"Fulton County Jail, ma'am. And you can call him."

The detective unlocked one hand and gave her the cordless phone from the desk. She dialed the only number that was committed to memory.

"David, this is Lyric. Pleasure Palate just got raided. Meet me on Rice Street. And call Roman for me, please."

"Gotcha. I'm on my way."

Breathing a sigh of relief, she put the phone down. David knew exactly what to do. He used to handle all her dad's business affairs.

"Do you need to make another call? I'm Detective Mowry, by the way."

"Nah, I'm good." She sat back and stared at him as he wrote something on a pad.

If he were not arresting her and she was not with Roman, she would have given this man the time of day. He was about five-eleven with a muscular build and his smooth skin was complimented by a perfectly trimmed goatee. For a white guy, he could definitely get it. But she had a good man and regardless of what trouble she faced, he would be by her side. A cop escorted Lyric to a squad car.

When they hit the door, cameras were shoved in her face and flashes went off.

"Why is the news here and how in the hell did they know to come?" She asked, shielding her face.

"Someone tipped'em off. I'm not surprised."

He may not have been, but she was. Who could have known that this was going to happen today? And how did Pleasure Palate get on the cop's radar?

I need my man here with me, she thought sadly as the car pulled away from the curb, headed toward the jail.

"**I** need you, baby. Put that big dick in my ass the way I like it." Alexis purred as Roman eased up behind her. He positioned himself at her tight opening, saturating his dick with saliva before ramming it inside.

"Damn. Eat Amber's pussy while I hit this," he commanded through grunts.

Amber moved over on the bed and slid down just enough for Alexis's mouth to reach her hot box. Lexi licked the young girl's clit like a kitten lapping at milk. Moans and heavy breathing came from all three.

"Mmm, right there, Daddy. That's my spot."

Roman fingered Alexis with three fingers and rubbed her clit with his thumb. The fire he ignited within her was about to combust. His own release was imminent. Involuntary movements in his pelvis caused him to thrust faster, harder. Muscle tension in his groin made the nerve endings in his hard shaft more sensitive and his heart rate increased. At the point-of-no-return, he pumped aggressively as his penis began a series of rapid-fire contractions. Hot semen poured out of him and into Lexi at the same time her creamy juices ran down her thigh. Amber gyrated her pelvis against her lovers' lips after she found her g-spot, until she too, erupted in pleasure.

Collapsing on the bed, the threesome lay intertwined, dozing off to sleep for a few moments. Shrill ringing awakened them.

"RJ here," he answered. "What? When?" My God, this is horrible. My flight just landed," he lied. "Let me get my bags and I'll meet David there. Thanks for calling me." He ended the call and smiled.

"Who was that babe?" Amber asked sweetly. Lexi rolled her eyes. She hated sharing her man with the young vixen.

"David's secretary telling me Pleasure Palate was raided by GBI. Lyric's in jail."

He rolled over and kissed Amber hard on the mouth. "You did it, babe, "he said, swatting her ass.

"Don't you mean, *we* did it?" Alexis corrected.

"Yeah. I gotta go." He went to shower. Lexi followed him.

"Why are you leaving now?" She was pissed off.

"Come off it. This is not over. It is just beginning. I told you that this is going to take some time and will not happen overnight. We all have roles to play. You two have done your parts, now it's time I do mine."

The loud rushing of water tuned her out. She sucked on her teeth and stomped off. In record time he dressed and headed toward downtown Atlanta. The hotel he had been at all weekend was by the airport. Only Alexis, Amber and the hotel staff who checked him in knew that he did not go to Miami.

By the time he got to the jail, David was there, and Lyric's and her staff's bonds had been posted.

"What is going on, Dave? Thanks for having your secretary call me. I got here as soon as I could."

David Burgen hated Roman and especially hated being called Dave. He rolled his eyes.

"Glad you decided to answer your phone," he replied. "I've taken care of everything. Lyric, Bella, Melody and Quad will be released within the hour. Lyric faces the most serious charges. The other's, misdemeanor prostitution. I suggest you work to get them acquitted first, that way you can build your defense for her."

Her case moved quickly. Once released, she immediately prepared for her defense. Human trafficking was not a charge to play with. The district attorney offered her a plea deal, but she was not willing to plead guilty or no contest. Her only option was to take it to trial, so she did.

Her defense team was solid with Roman at the helm. All too soon, her day in court was upon her.

"Good morning, ladies and gentlemen. Calling the case of the People of the State of Georgia versus Carter. Are both sides ready?"

The trial got under way. The prosecution had a confidential informant who claimed to have been threatened by someone from Lyrics camp. Because of that, the judge ruled that that person's sworn testimony statement would be admissible, and they would not have to appear in person. Her team would not have the opportunity to cross examine the person. The chips were stacked against her.

The prosecution was aggressive. One month after her arrest, both sides rested their cases and the jury went out to deliberate. They were gone less than half-an-hour.

"Will the jury foreperson please stand? Has the jury reached a unanimous verdict?"

"Yes, Your Honor."

The clerk took the folded paper from the woman and handed it to the judge. He read it silently before handing it back to the clerk so that it could be read to the court.

"Madam foreperson, what say you?"

"On count one, human trafficking, we the jury find the defendant...not guilty."

Cheers erupted in the courtroom. The judge banged his gavel.

Lyric breathed a sigh of relief.

"Order. Count two?" He said.

"On count two, felony pandering, we the jury find the defendant...guilty."

Lyric shrieked and tears ran slowly down her face.

The foreperson continued reading. "On count three, pimping under-aged participants, we the jury find the defendant…guilty."

The sound of camera's clicking, and chatter filled the galley.

"Order in the court. Lyric Elaine Carter, you have been found guilty by a jury of your peers. Sentencing will commence two-weeks from today. The jury is thanked and excused. Court is adjourned."

Chapter 4

A five-year prison sentence. Two to serve, three on probation. Had anyone told Lyric five months ago that she would be standing by a bunk on a prison yard, preparing for count, she would have called them everything but a child of God. But here she was. At the Bessie Glover Correctional Facility, they counted inmates five times between seven in the morning and ten at night and hourly overnight.

"This shit is for the birds," Lyric said, agitated after she sat on her bunk.

"Who are you telling?" Chantal, her bunkmate, and friend, said.

The day that she got on the yard, Lyric was scared and nervous as hell. Chantal was the first person she met, and she turned out to be cooler than a fan. They became fast friends, something that neither expected. Because she believed she was set-up, she was leery of trusting people. But for some reason, she trusted Chantal. It was as if she had known her a lifetime. The two were even closer than she and Alexis, whom she *had* known her entire life.

Subsequently, her childhood friend had only visited her in prison once, and that was a few weeks after she hit the yard. Since all this began, the relationship between the two of them was strained. One thing Lyric was learning the hard way is that people changed up on you fast once you were no longer able to help them. Nevertheless, Roman was there for her and he was all she needed.

"If count does not clear soon, I'm going to miss my appointment time at the beauty shop. Ro is coming to see me tomorrow and I want to look good."

"You really need to leave that creamy crack alone. Natural is the way to go."

"That is easy for you to say, Chan. You're Seminole with your Mulan looking ass."

"Mulan was Chinese."

"Whatever. I like getting perms. My hair is better managed with one. I just hate that we cannot perm our own hair. It's a headache having to buy a perm then send it to the prison beauty shop to have it stored."

"Yeah, that doesn't make any sense. We can buy razors and keep them in our property but not perms. Retarded."

The two continued to talk about the stupid rules until count cleared thirty-minutes later. Both worked in food service and had to return to their work assignments immediately. Mister Gandy, their supervisor, had given Lyric permission to get her hair done. Like most men, she had him wrapped around her finger. She was blessed with the gift of gab just like her daddy. That is what made him such a strong pimp and her such a powerful businesswoman.

There was not a man she encountered in her short twenty-seven years of living that she could not sway with her silver tongue and round ass. Her country bumpkin boss was more susceptible to her wiles because the only time he ventured out of the small town of Waycross, Georgia where he grew up was to go to Atlanta.

Big Honey, the inmate beautician who was assigned to do Lyrics hair, was the best on the yard. Prior to getting locked up, she sold drugs to make money. Her reading level was that of a third grader, so finding a job was difficult for her on the streets. She made ends meet by hustling rocks and running a kitchen beauty salon. With no family on the street to help support her, she stayed on the indigent list in the facility, so she could get a free hygiene kit monthly and a small stationary packet. The first time she did Lyrics hair, it was done so well that Lyric vowed to take care of her, and she had.

"My boo is coming to see me, Honey. Make it nice," she asked.

Two-hours later, she walked into the chow hall, looking like a million bucks. Chantal rushed over to her friend and gushed.

"Bitch, Honey outdid herself. This shit is silky. Is it Brazilian?" She joked.

"Only the best for me."

They laughed and began wiping the tables down. By the time the staff came in, the dining area was clean, and the food was done.

"Fuck, who is that?" Chantal asked, biting her fist.

"That's the new warden," Veronica, one of their friends said.

"Wow. He is sexy as hell."

"You got a hottie, Lyric. Leave some for the rest of us," Levia, another inmate said.

The small group was inseparable. They shared the same dorm, same work detail, and participated in activities together.

"Whatever, girl. Ain't no harm in looking."

"Not at all. I would suck his dick raw and swallow all his babies."

"Only you would say something like that, Levia," Chantal laughed.

"Ahem, if you have time to lean, you have time to clean," Mister Gandy said. "Get to work."

The ladies pretended to work as the staff found their seats and were served. Warden Fletcher stood head and shoulders above everyone who came in with him. Lyric could not help but notice how sexy his lips were, even from a distance. There was more than one feature that made him handsome. His hazel brown eyes were among that number and they held her captive. She managed to take her eyes off his face and looked at his big hands. They looked like they could pick her up and throw her on the bed and...she grimaced and shook her head to rid it of the provocative thoughts.

You have a man who comes to see you weekly. Snap out of it.

The warden looked across the room and saw the pretty inmate staring at him. Warden Fletcher recognized the look in Lyrics eyes as one he had seen many times before. Crazy thing is, he never cared until now. When he toured the yard the other day, he saw her working out in the commons. Her hair was pulled up into a ponytail, allowing him to see her smooth caramel skin that glistened with sweat. She ran around the track, breasts and ass bouncing as her feet hit the pavement. Sweat made the cotton top cling to her body like a wet t-shirt. Seeing her now, only confirmed his belief that she was a true beauty. Even the dingy, white kitchen uniform she wore, did little to mask the sexiness that emanated from her.

"Take this pitcher of water to the warden," Mister Gandy told Lyric.

Exhaling, she took it and walked over and placed it on the table.

"Here you go, Sir. Anything else?" She was happy that he sat alone because she was thirsty but not for water.

"No. Thank you. What's your name?"

"Carter. Lyric Carter." Smiling, she turned to leave. "Enjoy your meal."

That night, lying on her bunk, it was the warden's face, not her man's, that she saw before drifting off to sleep. The following morning, she got up and dressed for her visit. While she loved seeing Ro, she hated the process that ensued after the visits. Inmates underwent a strip search. They had to squat, spread their butt cheeks and cough, to ensure they did not have anything in their body cavities. It was tedious, but to see her man, she would endure that plus a whole lot more.

Heads turned as usual when he walked in the room. Roman was the best-dressed, best looking man in the room. She was the envy of all the inmates, and they were the talk of the yard.

"Hey, love," he said, kissing her deeply.

"Hey. I missed you."

"Not more than I missed you."

They exchanged pleasantries and talked about what was going on in the streets for a while.

"Put your hand under the table, babe," she said, not taking her eyes off his.

He did as he was told. She took his hand and guided it to the hole in her pants.

"Oh," he said. His fingers slid easily inside her smooth, clean shaven pussy. "You are so wet."

"All for you baby," she said. Covering his hand with the tail of her shirt, she pushed his fingers deeper inside, gasping softly as his middle finger curled upwards, toward her g-spot.

She moved forward, balancing on the edge of her chair, spreading her legs wider, to give him better access. He leaned in to kiss her.

"Hmm," she moaned sweetly into his mouth. She feigned a stretch, so she could move her hips to the beat of the finger-fucking he was giving her. It was hard for her to concentrate on keeping her face expressionless and her breathing even, as his long fingers penetrated her. They were slick with her nectar.

"You know I love you, right?" He asked her.

"Mmm hmm," she said softly.

In one movement, his fingers went as deeply as they could. She was on the brink of eruption. Her pussy tightened around him and began contracting as her hot juices flowed from her center. The quiet, yet powerful orgasm robbed her of her strength. Roman licked the nectar from his fingers just as the end of visitation was called. He kissed her, allowing her to taste herself on his lips. Neither could wait for the next visit.

Chapter 5

Roman's hard dick sprang to life when Alexis bounced her heart-shaped ass in front of him to the beat of one of Drake's songs. She turned and slowly walked her curvy, naked body to the bed. The mattress dipped slightly under the weight of her as she crawled toward his stiff rod. She leaned forward and grabbed his thick meat. A drop of pre-cum glistened at the tip and she licked it off.

Caressing it slowly, she drew it closer and closer to her mouth. Soon she was stroking it with both hands and rubbing it all over her face, eventually bringing it to her mouth. Opening wide, she amazed him by taking the entire sausage into her mouth without hesitation, making it completely disappear. Holding it in her throat, she swallowed and heard Roman grunt.

"Ah, shit," he moaned as she bobbed up and down.

"Make it wet," he said.

Like the pro she was, Alexis salivated all over his shaft, rubbing him with her hands as she did so.

"Fuck, this shit feels good. Lyric never sucked me off like this." There was a devilish grin on Roman's face when he said that. Lexi was always trying to outdo Lyric in one way or the other. Truth is, Lyric never sucked his dick at all. She did not give head.

Looking into his eyes, she smiled and rolled her tongue over the tip of the head. Like a lollipop she sucked and savored him, clamping her jaws down on his hard dick. From base to tip, she caressed him with her tongue. Of course, her friend never did it like this. Lexi was a pro at giving head. Hell, she had even taught a few of the girls at Pleasure Palate how to properly suck dick and even how to trick the gag reflex.

"Mmm, you like this baby?"

"Hell, yeah," he replied, placing both of his hands on the back of her head.

Changing places, Roman's tongue dived deep into her dripping pussy and Alexis moaned in delight as it happened. She grabbed Roman's head and pulled it tightly into her, her hips now pumping in time with the thrusting tongue inside her.

"Come on, boo. Give me that ass," he demanded.

She reluctantly moved his head and turned over.

"Shove that big dick in my dookie shoot and fuck me silly!"

"Damn!" He exclaimed and began pumping away.

Every powerful thrust drove deeper inside Alexis's asshole. Using her middle finger, she stretched her arm between her legs and began to rub her clitoris. Her legs trembled as tiny pulsating shocks began to travel upwards to her hot center. A few long strokes later from behind and she had a mind-numbing orgasm. Within moments his rhythm grew ragged and with a bellow, he thrust his meat as far into her as he could and began to pump his white lava deep inside her.

"I swear your shit gets tighter each time we fuck," he commented.

"Hmm, maybe." Her tone was noncommittal, and her face gave nothing away.

"What's wrong now?" He exhaled hard, rolling his eyes in the top of his head.

"I don't want to put on a waist cincher, so I'm not going to go visit Lyric today."

Slap! Roman smacked her face so hard, it stung.

"Your ass will do what the fuck I say, when I say it."

Hot tears ran down her face and into her ears as she lay on her back crying.

"It's not good for the baby, Roman. I'm pregnant."

"Do I look like I give a fuck about that? We must get those papers signed, today. Understand me?"

She nodded. This was not the first time that he admitted he cared little for their child. Since she told him that she was pregnant he acted nonchalantly. Last year, when Lyric told him that she *thought* she was pregnant, he went out and bought cigars before it was even confirmed. When the test came back negative, he took it harder than anyone. With her, he was the opposite. Even after she told him about the baby, he still asked her friend to marry him and that was not part of the plan.

Lexi had fallen in love with Roman even before he stepped to her about a scheme. She felt that he may be taking advantage of her feelings for him and using them to get what he wanted. But blinded by her love for him, she did not care. They were together and that was all that mattered. A part of her knew that he was really in love with her friend, but she did not care about that either. She would rather have a piece of him than none at all.

"Get up and get dressed. I do not want to be late."

Once he heard the spray of the shower, Roman picked up the phone and made a call.

"Hey, Misses Jones. How are you?"

"I'm fine, honey. What's up?"

"Getting ready to go see Lyric and get those papers signed. You are about to become one of the richest women in Atlanta. You ready?"

Amber giggled on the other end. "Of course, I am, silly. That is what all this has been for right? Me, you and our family."

"You got that right. I cannot wait to see you swollen with my baby. When this is all over, we are fucking like rabbits until I get you pregnant."

"No complaints here. You know I love how your big dick feels in this pussy."

"Damn, my dick just got hard. I love it when you talk like that."

"Go take a shower and handle that. Call me after the visit and let me know how it went."

"Will do. Love you."

"Love you, too."

His dick was standing at attention, but instead of whacking it himself, he went to the shower with Alexis. He stepped in, lifted her leg to the edge of the tub and slid inside her, pumping roughly. Painfully, he squeezed her breasts between thrusts, all the while imagining that it was his wife, Amber that he was fucking.

Pen Pals

Roman was the Master of Games. Not only had he convinced Lyric that he loved her, he managed to do the same thing to Alexis. Soon it would all be his and everything he worked hard for, would be complete. He could not wait until the day he could tell his father that the plan they came up with so long ago, paid off.

The line of visitors was long when they arrived at the prison. Thankfully, he used his attorney privilege and was escorted through another door. Alexis was on the record as his paralegal and was granted the same access.

"How do I look?" She asked nervously, turning around so he could see her from different angles.

"Damn, that's a tight ass cincher. Your stomach is almost as flat as it was before the baby."

"I know. I am glad I am not that big. This shit is uncomfortable, but I will live. Visiting hours are not that long anyway."

"That's my girl."

They were seated as inmates began making their way into the visiting room. All of them were excited and walked quickly to their visitors. When Lyric walked in, the first-person she saw was Alexis. Her pace slowed the closer she got.

"What are you doing here?"

Expecting this type of reception, Lexi prepared an act for this very moment. Tears welled in her eyes.

"I know you may not want to see me, but I love you. I'm ashamed that I wasn't there for you, but I was scared."

"Scared of what? I'm the one who's locked up."

"That's just it. I had a nightmare about Techwood and was terrified that I would lose you like we did him. You are all the family I have, Lily," she said, using the nickname she had given her as a child. "Plus, I was embarrassed for a while because the guy I was messing with beat me up and my face was swollen for almost a month. How could I face you?"

"A nigga beat you up? Who is this cat? Is it the bastard I heard you arguing with in the office that day?"

"Huh? You heard me arguing on the phone?"

"Uh, yeah. But that was so long ago."

With downcast eyes, Lexi said, "no, this guy and I only dated a few months. He's in jail now."

"I'm so glad you are okay."

"Awe, group hug," Roman said, and they all embraced.

They sat and chatted like old times. When they got hungry, they got food out the vending machines. Lyric's hands were busy cutting up the microwaveable burrito she bought. Under the table, Roman's hands were busy searching for the hole in her pants.

"Oh, before I forget, I have some papers for you to sign."

"What are they?" She asked.

"Bank of Georgia is changing their name. It's just an acknowledgement saying that you understand none of your banking products will change."

"I need to read them over," she said.

Alexis laughed and began to talk about the stud that had just walked into the visiting room.

"There's you a woman right there, Sis." She said.

"Nah, I got this," Roman said, finding her spot. He rubbed her clit softly and whispered, "It's all good. Just sign them. It is nothing. Damn, babe I wish we could make love."

Pen Pals

His middle finger penetrated her pussy and he fucked her with one finger. She could not think straight. Alexis slid an ink pen across the table. Lyrics breathing became shallow as her insides heated up. Faster, Roman rubbed, helping her reach her peak. The pen was poised over the signature. Using his free hand, it pushed it down on the paper. Just as she was cumming on his finger, Lyric signed on the dotted line. He removed his finger and licked the juice off. Alexis smiled. Once he filed the papers in the Fulton County court, Carter Holdings would belong to her.

Chapter 6

yric's time sheet was messed up. The unit manager, Miss Crosby, sat at her desk surfing the web and could care less about anything that the women on her unit had going on. If there were prisoners there, she had a job. They were job security for her.

Tap, tap, tap, Lyric knocked. "May I come in?"

The woman exhaled loudly. "What now, Carter? I'm busy."

"I can see how difficult it must be to find a swimsuit in your size that is both flattering and sexy, so I will make this quick and let you get back to your pressing work," she said sarcastically. "My time sheet is wrong. It only shows that I completed one-hundred thirty days."

The case manager snatched the paper from Lyric and scanned it.

"It is correct," she said, throwing it back to her.

"No, it is not. I got on this yard, April thirteenth. My time started that day. I'm missing forty days from that, plus you did not give me credit for the regimented training program I completed which took off an additional one-hundred twenty days."

Pen Pals

"Are you saying I do not know how to do my job?"

"Nope. But I am saying you do not know how to count."

"Get the hell out my office before I write you up for disrespect to staff."

Lyric turned on her heels and left. She would work it out on her own. If all else failed, she would call David and ask him to fix it. *There is no way I am getting fucked out of my time she thought*, heading to work before the yard closed.

"Hey, booski. What did Miss Crows Feet say?" Levia asked when she walked in.

"Girl let me tell you about this bitch. She said that my time was correct."

"How she figure? Did you show her when you got here and all that?"

"Everything. It did not matter that old goat. If I do not get the days that are owed to me, that will delay me going home."

"Awe, don't cry boo bear." Tears welled in the corners of Lyrics eyes and Levia leaned over to hug her.

The kitchen supervisor walked in the door and the warden was behind him.

"What is going on, Carter? Why are you crying?"

Levia walked off and left Lyric alone to explain her dilemma. The time sheet was still in her pocket, so she used it to plead her case.

"Don't fret. I will make a copy of your time sheet and see what I can do. Until then, get to work and let's get ready for lunch."

Chantal came around the corner with a small bucket of hot, sudsy water but stopped when she saw her friend.

"What are you getting ready to do?" Lyric asked her.

"I was going to wipe down tables until I saw my sexy man over there. I need him to scratch this itch I have for him."

"Hmph. The only thing he can do for me is fix my time, so I can blow this joint when it is time," Lyric told her friend.

"Whatever. Help me wipe these tables," Chantal asked.

Lyric agreed, grabbing a dry cloth. She dipped her towel in the water and began wiping down tables. The table next to the warden's was dirty so she cleaned it.

"Miss Carter, you are too cute to work in this kitchen," he flirted.

"Puppies are cute, Warden Fletcher. I am beautiful," she retorted. "And if you feel that way, you are in position to change my work assignment." She gave him a fake smile and sauntered off.

"Yes, ma'am you are very beautiful," he agreed quietly. Golden bronzed skin, full luscious, pouty lips and piercing dark brown eyes, were the first things he noticed about her. The fat ass and small waist on her short, five-feet-two-inch frame were the second. She was correct, he did have the authority to do something about her work detail, so he did.

The next week she found herself working in the administration building where his office was located. For her, it was a welcomed change. No more aches and pains that came after lifting a sixty-quart mixing bowl from the floor mixer to the sink to wash it. Or her skin peeling from being submerged in chemical-filled dishwater all day. Shuffling papers, emptying waste baskets and dusting shelves was nothing compared to all that. Having worked in foodservice for so long, Lyric knew all the staff there and they loved her. Especially the warden's secretary.

Pen Pals

Misses Elnora, the warden's assistant was old, and hard of hearing. She spoke extremely loudly when giving Lyric instructions. Not only that, she was legally blind in one eye. The woman had it bad, but she was sweet as pie. Noticing that Lyric could type and knew her way around an office, the older woman asked her to start helping with light clerical duties. Shortly thereafter, she ended up doing things for the warden directly. Immediately after she started working for him, he told her that he would help her fix her time and he was true to his word. It had been a long time since she had met someone as genuine as him and let her guard down around him. As a result, the two of them talked daily, getting to know one another.

Denim Fletcher. A sexy ass name for a sexy ass man. The more Lyric talked to him the more she wanted to. He challenged her to think when they spoke. Intellect was stimulating and turned her on.

"Was your father a musician the reason he chose your name?"

"No, he was a pim- I mean, businessman, like me."

Although he smiled, he gathered she was serious.

"My daddy named me Lyric, because he said that when the doctor told them that he and my mom were having a daughter, it was music to his ears."

"Most men want sons first, so they can carry on the family name and help protect the family."

"Techwood, was not most men and I believe that he knew as his daughter, I would not be like most women," she finished softly.

He stared at her. She blushed and looked away. The sexual tension was so thick it could be cut with a knife. For the past few weeks that she had worked in his office, thoughts of them together filled her head. Even when Roman visited the other day, she could not help but feel indifferent toward him. Things had changed between her and her man and honestly, she did not care. Not that she was making plans to be with the warden, as if it were even possible, but she felt that she was changing in a way that would render her and Roman's relationship null and void by the time she was released.

"Life is short, Lyric. We do not always get a second chance at certain opportunities. At the risk of sounding cliché, I want you to know that I do not ever do this."

"Do what?"

She looked up just as he stood before her.

"This."

Slowly, he leaned is six-foot-three-inch frame down and covered her mouth with his. Their tongues intertwined in an erotic dance that caused hot moisture to pool between her pussy lips. A dull ache pulsated in his groin. He needed her closer. Long arms reached around her back and lifted her into the air. She wrapped her short, strong thighs around his waist and held on for the ride.

Denim walked to the office door and twisted the lock before sitting in a chair at his desk. Lyric was positioned on top of a large, hard bulge that had formed in his pants. One she could not help but appreciate. An itch between her nether lips began and she rubbed against him trying to scratch it. The clothes restricted her.

"I need you," she admitted.

"You got me."

Without taking their eyes off one another, they stood and quickly undressed.

"Wow," Lyric said, admiring the washboard abs and thick muscular thighs he had.

"My sentiments exactly."

Repeating what he did earlier, Denim lifted her off her feet and she wrapped her legs around him. With his hands cupping her ass cheeks, he shifted her until her wet womanhood was poised at the tip of his stiff dick. Unable to restrain himself any longer, he penetrated her opening.

"Ah," he exhaled in pleasure.

Thrusting upward, he pumped in a steady rhythm trying to find her g-spot.

"Yes, baby," she moaned. Both of her hands were on his shoulders and she used them to help her rise and fall on his manhood.

His knees wobbled when a powerful orgasm began to form. Carefully, he laid her down on the carpeted floor behind his desk. The solid surface was exactly what he needed to give it to her the way he wanted to. Deep, long strokes sent her spiraling out of control as she clawed at his ass.

"Right. There." Her words were choppy. Speaking was not possible, nor was it necessary.

Downward stroke. Upward stroke. Power stroke. Like a piston, Denim gave her the best of him until his engine began to overheat.

"I'm cumming," he said, trying to pull out. But she was cumming, too and held him in place. Electric pulses traveled up his toes and through his loins as he spilled his seed inside her. A gushing of juices flowed from her as spasms overtook her.

Heavy breathing filled the air. Their bodies were moist with perspiration. No time to linger and revel in their love making, they dressed quickly.

"I'm serious. I have never stepped to an inmate or any woman on my job before."

"And I have never banged a warden before. Can't believe I did it now."

He stood within inches of her face, lifted her chin with his index finger and kissed her.

"From the moment I laid eyes on you, I have desired you. I promise, you are the only woman I want from now on. And I do not know how I am going to make it happen, but next time, I am going to make it good."

Her body was still responding to the loving he had just given her and from all accounts, it was damned good.

Her chin touched her chest as she buttoned her uniform. "So that was considered bad in your book?"

"Not bad, but it could be better."

"Damn."

"Look, we are both in a precarious situation but there's something between us that needs to be explored."

She felt it, also. It was not just physical either. He had gotten into her head, just like a pimp. And if she were not careful, he would take over her heart, if he had not already.

"So, what are we going to do?"

Denying him anything was pointless because she wanted, no she needed him, as much as he needed her.

"I have not forgotten that you have a man."

It is good that he did not because she certainly did.

"Yeah."

Pen Pals

"Are you in love with him?"

"We have been together four years. I love him."

"That's not what I asked."

"Isn't it the same thing?" She shrugged.

"No. Looks like I am going to have to teach you the difference."

And just like that, class was in session.

Chapter 7

Something must have happened because when Lyric found Levia, Chantal and Veronica sitting at a table by the education building, their shoulders were slumped, their heads hung low and Levia's face was wet with tears.

"Who died?" She asked, before sitting down.

"Nobody, but Levia and Veronica got some bad news."

"What's going on Lee?"

Tearfully, the woman explained how her boyfriend's elderly aunt was sick and could no longer care for her three-year-old son, Parker.

And no one on her side of the family was willing to take him in.

"Not even your mother?" Lyric shook her head in disbelief. It was hard to fathom a grandmother turning away her grandchild who really needed her.

"Nope. Especially not her."

"What about his cousin, Robin? Can she take him?"

She shook her head. "She would take him but shit, she has six kids and barely making ends meet as it is. Right now, he is with her, but I do not know how long that's going to last."

Except for Chantal, each lady at the table had been dealt some sort of blow.

"Veronica why are you down?"

"My sister Vicky lost her job a few months ago, Lyric. Normally she would have one by now, but it is tough out there. The house payment is behind and if she does not make a payment by the end of next month, the bank will begin foreclosure proceedings."

"Damn and I thought Roman's not coming to visit for a while was bad but it's nothing compared to these things."

"He's not? Why?" Chantal asked.

She told them about the phone conversation the two of them just had. Apparently, one of his clients was facing some serious charges in another state and he needed to be there for him. Lyric knew him well and could hear the deception in his voice. Whatever reason he had for not coming to see her was fine. Since she had been messing with Denim, Roman was the last thing on her mind anyway. Same with Alexis. That may have been her best friend since childhood but not as adults. There were times she doubted that Lexi liked her, let alone loved her. Being locked up taught her the hard way who was for her and who was against her.

The women continued talking for another hour before going to the dorm. Although it was October, it was hot outside and the sun had Lyric's gray shirt and pants clinging to her body and she needed a shower. She sat on the edge of her metal bed and removed her sneakers and socks and slipped on a pair of shower shoes.

Hygiene bag in tow, she made her way to the shower. There was a large stall that all the women tried to get to first because it was set up for a disabled person. It had a bench and handrail, making it easy for women to shave their legs. Unfortunately, it was taken so she used the one across from it.

She stepped inside and pulled the shower curtain closed. It was made from the same hard, pea green colored plastic that they used to cover the mattresses the women slept on. The water came out cold, making Lyric jump out of shock, causing the curtain to open slightly. Just as she was about to close it, she heard a moan. Nosey, she moved the curtain slightly and peered into the stall across the way. She could see a chick named Dana, with her head thrown back and her girlfriend, Navajo, was sucking on her neck.

Damn, they are getting it in. So that she would not be caught spying on them, she opened her curtain another inch but backed up into the corner of her shower, allowing the darkness to shield her. The curtain across from her opened a tad bit more. Lyric watched in fascination as the Native-American woman plunged her tongue into her girlfriends' mouth. Strangely, she got turned on by watching the two inmates kiss. Hot moisture pooled between her lips.

Moans of pleasure escaped the women's throats. Dana sat on the bench and opened her legs so that her girlfriend could ease her hand between her thighs. In and out, long fingers   manipulated her pussy. Because most of her body was hidden behind the curtain, Lyric did not see Navajo get on her knees, all she saw was the woman's head as it nestled between her lover's thighs. Hungrily, she lapped at the juices that she created while her girlfriend held her head steady. Turned on, Lyric slid two fingers between her lips, stroking herself, imagining that it was Denim who was fucking her.

Even though the water streamed loudly, she heard a soft moan but was surprised because it came from her.

Her walls were slippery, and her fingers created friction like two sticks being rubbed together. Heat permeated her center and her nipples were rock hard and sensitive. She rubbed them, watching as Dana's hips gyrated on the bench. Lost in her own passion, Lyric added another finger, stretching her pussy and going deeper. She bit her lower lip to suppress another moan as she rolled her nipple between her thumb and index finger. Pressure began to build within her. She saw Dana stand and turn around, placing her hands on the wall in front of her.

What in the hell? Lyric watched incredulously as Navajo stood behind Dana, impaling her with a long, thick, home-made, dildo. Back and forth, using long strokes, the stud filled her girlfriend's pussy up. Missing the D, Lyric added another finger to the action, but this one, slid into her ass. She began fucking both holes, moving at the same pace as the lesbians across from her. Pressure mounted inside and became almost unbearable. Like a starburst, Lyric came quietly and slid down the wall, never taking her eyes off the action.

"I'm about to bust," she heard Navajo say. Pumping vigorously, Lyric giggled quietly as Dana bumped her head against the wall. She moaned loudly. Too loud.

"What's going on in here?" The C.O. on duty said, busting in the shower room.

Lyric scrambled to her feet just in time to see the woman pull the curtain back on the lesbian lovers, catching them in the act.

"Well congratulations, Miss Wyatt, you just earned yourself a Class A Sexual Misconduct. I guess you won't be going home next week."

The woman came to Lyrics stall and pulled her curtain back as well. The only thing she saw was Lyric bathing. Alone.

"May I help you?" She asked the guard, whose gaze lingered on her naked body.

"Rinse off and clear out, Carter, unless you want to go to the SHU with your buddies here."

As she exited the shower room, two brawny female officers came with shackles to escort the lovers to the segregated housing unit. Dana was scheduled to be released in just five short days, but thanks to the write-up she would receive, her release date would be pushed back almost a year.

Damn, Lyric thought. *She is going to have a helluva time to explaining that to her kids. And her husband.*

The next day, she took extra care getting ready for work. Even though there was nothing she could do to alter the unflattering uniform, she made sure it was pressed well. Also, she flat ironed her hair and paid more attention to her makeup. It was important for her to look good for her boss. She gave herself a final once over and walked across the yard to the administrative offices.

"Hello, Miss Carter," Elnora said. "I was just about to page you. Warden Fletcher needs to see you."

Page her? For what? Shrugging her shoulders, she walked toward his door.

"Go in, dear," the older woman instructed.

Taking a deep breath, she twisted the knob and walked in. Her plan was to walk straight up to him and kiss him.

Instead, she stopped short when she saw David seated across from the man who had been her lover for the past month.

"David, what are you doing here?"

Denim stood up and walked around his desk. "He called me regarding an urgent matter. Have a seat, babe."

Her eyes darted from Denim to David. It did not escape her notice that he called her 'babe' in the presence of someone who was there on official business.

"Relax, little one. Warden Fletcher…Denim and I have spoken candidly. We have an understanding. Sit."

She nodded and sat down, wringing her hands nervously. David shuffled some papers in his briefcase before pulling some out. He handed them to her.

"Do you recognize any of these documents?"

They looked vaguely familiar. "Um, yeah. These are the documents that Roman brought for me to sign from the bank about the new name."

"Okay. What about this one?" He pulled one from the bottom of the stack.

"I've never seen this before." A sinking feeling developed in the pit of her stomach.

"Is this your signature?" The question was redundant.

She gulped. "Yes. What's going on?"

"This is a document giving Alexis Murray full power-of-attorney for Carter Holdings. She and Roman liquidated your assets. They took everything associate with it. Not the family home though. That's still intact."

"You're kidding right?" Her legs felt like lead and she could not move.

Denim walked to her and put his arms around her as she sat.

"It's serious, Lyric. You are broke babe. He also removed himself as attorney-of-record on your file and had this sent to my office. As warden, I must abide by it."

This turned out to be a formal request made by Roman to the warden to restrict any communication between him and Lyric.

"Those punk ass bitches. I knew something was going on. Fuck!"

David sat and watched the warden comfort his client, who cried in his arms. Sobs racked her body. Just as quickly as the tears began, they stopped. Lyric threw her head back and wiped her face.

"I've got to make some money, so I can hire someone to help me get my money back. I'm not taking no L's for nobody."

Her business manager saw a fire light in her eyes and understood it to mean that she meant business.

"Taking losses is not your style. I have got to get out of here but just so you know, I am going to work on getting your assets back. Call me if you need me." David gave her a tight hug of reassurance before he left.

"I am here to help you also, babe if you need me." Denim kissed her forehead and she walked back to her dorm, in a daze.

That night, lying on her bunk, she began to put a plan together. The events of the day were nerve-racking for her and all her friends. Before she drifted off to sleep, Lyric developed two plans. The first to help her and her friends make money. And the second one was how to get away with Roman and Alexis's murder.

Chapter 8

He was hard and ready lying on the bed beside her. Lyric gently brushed her fingertips up the shaft of his penis and enjoyed watching it bounce excitedly. Drops of pre-cum gleamed at the top of his dick after teasing it that way. Salivating over the head, she lubricated his weapon and stroked it with her tiny hand. His back arched, and eyes rolled in pleasure. She smiled… a tingle stirred in her clit.

"Ah," he gasped.

Her tongue swirled over the head as her hand continued its movement. She lowered her mouth over the shiny tip, taking him slowly into her mouth. Applying gentle pressure with her mouth, she sucked and raised up. When her mouth came off his rod, it made a 'pop' sound.

"Are you ready?" She asked him.

He did not use any words. Instead, he placed his hands on the back of her head to guide her up and down on his shaft. Like a vacuum, she sucked his dick, getting it wet with her saliva. She caressed his balls with her free hand, savoring the taste of him. Getting to her knees, without taking her mouth off him, she twisted around and straddled his face so that they were in a sixty-nine position. Strong hands grabbed her ass and held on as she lowered herself to his tongue.

The thick tongue felt like velvet, lapping at her juices. He licked the hard nub from under its hood, before gently sucking on it.

"Aye," she cried out. "Yes, baby."

The more he licked, the more she sucked. It was a tag team of pleasure. That is, until Denim inserted his thumb in her asshole. The move made her lose her breath and she stopped sucking immediately.

"Oh. My. Gosh. Mmm," she moaned in pleasure. On the verge of a powerful orgasm, she grinded her pelvis in his mouth. Sensations began to travel up her legs and her breathing got erratic. But just as she was about to cum, he stopped.

"I need to be inside you," he explained, flipping her over and easing between her thighs.

He gazed into her eyes and gave her a sweet, passionate kiss before entering her. Kisses rained over her neck and his hands kneaded her ample breasts.

"Denim," she whispered in his ear as he nuzzled her neck.

"Wet my dick," he said seductively.

The intense pleasure from earlier returned in her loins. This time, he stroked her to completion. He thrust a few times and her sugar walls clinched his manhood to send them both over the edge, his hot semen mixing with her creamy nectar. A passionate kiss followed their explosion and Denim rolled over onto his back.

"Warden Fletcher, that was hands-down the best loving I ever received."

Huffing and puffing, he said, "Man, that was bananas. And your tongue game…"

"So, I take it you liked it?"

"Like it? I loved it! Am I seriously the first man you've ever done this for?"

"Yes. The first and the last."

"Why me?"

"Because I love you and I want to please you like you do me."

"You love me?"

"Yep. I'm in love with you."

"How do you know?"

"Loving someone means wishing them well and wanting the best for them. That is true for me regarding you. But being in love with someone means putting them first at times and considering them all the time." She caressed his face. "I am in love with you Denim Michael Fletcher."

"And I'm in love with you, Lyric Elaine Carter."

"So, how much time do we have here?"

He rolled over and looked at the time on his cellphone.

"Another hour."

"Good. I want to ride your mechanical bull."

A half-hour later, she collapsed on his chest. Her index finger made circles around his nipple. A slow smile spread on her face as she thought about the lengths he had gone through to be with her today. Under the guise of going to court, Lyric was escorted off the compound by a U.S. Marshall, who was David's nephew. There were street clothes for her that she changed into. Liam drove them to a parking garage, where she exited the van and got into the car with Denim, who drove them to his sister's house. She remained in the car until he pulled into the garage and the door closed securely.

"This was a great idea. Whose plan was it?" She giggled.

"Mine and David's. The day he came to my office to tell me about your company, he read me like a book. There was no way I should care about what happened to you that much unless I cared about you, period. I figured if you trusted him as much as you did, then I could too, and I laid my cards on the table."

"I'm glad you did. Babe, I have an idea to help me recoup my loss and help my friends, also."

She inhaled and let the idea roll off her tongue. It was so preposterous to him that he had to sit up in bed.

"You want us to what?" He needed to hear her say it again because he was not sure he heard correctly the first time.

"Start an escort service at the prison. I even came up with a name for it... 'Pen Pals'. Catchy, huh?"

"You sure like the letter P for businesses, I see."

"Never thought of it, but it seems that way."

There were several details she had already worked out. The ladies would have a fake work assignment overnight. The warden could contact a few of Lyrics more prominent clientele and get them up to speed about her new business. To ensure the ladies were paid, an online bank account would be established in each of their names. A transaction for the service must clear the main account first and from there, either Denim or Lyric would transfer the money to the ladies' individual accounts.

"I know a man who owns a ranch thirty-miles north of here. Rusty, has a barn and house that's connected."

"And how do you know this?"

"He was one of my best clients, Denim. I'm sure he would be willing to help me."

"It seems like you have this all thought out. If I agree to this, what do you need me to do?"

Asking questions was always a good sign. That meant that there was some interest. All she had to do was go over the financials with him and she believed that he would be on board.

"Get the corrections department to approve the new work assignment. Once that is done, we are in business. Give me some time alone with your computer to set up accounts. Call David to let him know what I am up to. He will tell you how to proceed. Finally, be prepared to start making some serious money."

"Exactly how much money are we talking about here?"

"Well, had I not gotten busted, Pleasure Palate was set to make over a million-dollars for Valentine's Day and All-Star Weekend. And that was only using four of my best girls. Since it is a smaller scale, I'd say we can clear about ten to fifteen-thousand."

There were certain aspects about his past that Denim had not divulged to Lyric. But now was not the time. He enjoyed his job as warden, but he took this job to serve a bigger purpose. The money he received from Pen Pal's would come in handy.

"Hmmm, that's a nice piece of change for a month."

"Ha, ha, ha, ha." She laughed so hard; he took offense. "Not a month, a night," she corrected.

"Wow. That really puts things in perspective. But what if your old clientele wants no part of it? After all, they were placed in danger when you were busted. Things could have ended badly for them."

"My clients were protected. No one, not even Alexis knew their identity. When my files were confiscated, prosecutors were dumbfounded because they could not subpoena anyone."

"I read your case. Why did they charge you with human trafficking?"

"They jumped the gun on that charge and had to dismiss it. It would have been considered human trafficking had we done New York like I wanted to, because it's illegal to go from state to state with the purpose of commercial sexual exploitation."

They continued to discuss her case in-depth. The five-year sentence could have been worse because she was guilty, but it was still fishy. Everything happened so quickly she did not have the chance to breathe. Fortunately, it would all be over soon.

"We don't have that much time left. Let us make the most of it," he said.

His deep, soothing voice washed over her like a warm spring. The implications of what he had to offer, made her moist. Her legs spread almost involuntarily, welcoming him home. Long, nimble fingers rested at the opening of her hot slit. He slid one, then two inside, curling them upward, to tickle her g-spot. She began writhing in ecstasy, reveling in pleasure. Without removing his fingers, he slid down her body and sucked her clit.

"Ooh, baby," she purred like a kitten.

He was such a gentle, considerate lover, unlike Roman, who rushed through their foreplay at times, so he could get off as quickly as possible. No, Denim took his time, pleasing her which is why she discarded her hang-ups about giving him head.

"Slurp." The sounds of their lovemaking drove her wild.

Pressure mounted in his loins and his shaft was engorged. The relief he sought lie between her thighs. Skillfully, he moved between her legs and buried himself deep inside her. They had made love earlier, but right now, he needed to fuck her good. He grabbed her ass and lifted her hips, so he could pummel her pussy. It did not take long for either of them to reach their apex.

"Ahh," they both exhaled, breathing heavily.

After a quick shower, they redressed and prepared to head back to the parking garage so Liam could transport her back to the prison.

"One more thing. Who do you trust on the yard enough to help you pull off something like this?"

"I already have my crew. They are solid, just like me."

And all of them had so much more to lose than their freedom. Lyric had a game plan and they would help her carry it out.

Outside the prison walls, Roman had a plan, too. His was more self-serving. He sat in his South Beach condo, admiring his view from the twenty-seventh floor. Things were good and once he had this document signed; they were going to get a whole lot better.

"Lex, come here love."

She stood slowly, seductively, so he could ogle her goods. She had just come in from the pool and her bikini hugged her in all the right places. Her stomach was flat and tight, like it was before the baby.

"What is it, honey?" She leaned down and kissed his forehead.

"I need you to sign-off on a few things before we head to the airport."

He pulled her into his lap and began nibbling on her ear, handing her an ink pen. When she took it, he slid the papers in front of her, indicating where he needed her signature. His middle finger managed to ease inside her bikini bottom to find her warm cave. He rolled it around, and then moved it up and down, stroking her.

"Hurry up and sign, baby. I need you."

Quickly she scribbled her name on the forms so her man could give her something she could feel. Roman gave the papers a once over. Once satisfied, he picked her up and took her to the bed. Now, he had everything he needed, and Alexis had just given it to him because she was dick-stracted.

Chapter 9

ights out. Game on. Pen Pals was in business. Lyric was nervous. This was the first assignment for the ladies. The longevity of the business was predicated on tonight's success. They had to do well. It was not hard to get the ladies to sign on. As-a-matter of fact, it was easier than expected.

When she brought it up to Chantal in a round-about way, she was expecting for her friend to balk at the idea. The two were discussing money, or the lack thereof.

"Too bad I can't get an operation like Pleasure Palate going on here. Then we would be straight on funds."

"Hell, yeah," Chantal agreed. "I would sign-on in a heartbeat. All those broke ass bums I've fucked for free, might as well get something out of it."

The conversation pretty much went the same way with Levia. Her son was her 'why' though.

"If I did something like that, I could send money to Robin who would then be able to keep my baby. I would also have a little something, something put up for when I touched down."

Veronica was not hesitant, but she alluded to some debt on the yard that may pose an issue down the line. Lyric was a bit skeptical and asked her about it.

"You said you would take some money and pay your debts off here?" She repeated the question to be sure she heard correctly.

Veronica simply nodded.

"Who do you owe?"

"Jessie," she lied. Had she said Lady Tee, Veronica figured that Lyric would know the debt was drug related because that is all the brawny inmate dealt with. "I owe her for some quilts she made my sister that I sent out a month ago." That was her story and she was sticking to it.

Lyric gathered all the women together and they walked around the track. It was there that she told them the truth about Pen Pals and there that they made a vow of silence. Confidentiality was key. If they breached it, all of them could kiss their freedom goodbye and plan to spend half their lives in prison.

None of the women knew that Lyric would not be messing around with the clients. She did not want them to feel as if they were being pimped. They also did not know that Denim was involved. If things went bad, Lyric did not want him to be collateral damage. The officer that transported them was his friend and he felt the same way she did. The fewer people who knew all the players, the better.

A benefit with them not knowing he was involved was the fact that he was going to be right there with her. She could make love to her man five days a week. They would not have to worry about sneaking in a quickie in his office unless they wanted to. Now, they would have four hours each evening to enjoy one another's company.

"Listen up, guys. Tonight, each of us are set to make ten stacks each. Before you enter the room with your client, the money will be in your account. I cannot stress how important discretion is on our parts. When we hit that yard, we cannot go down to the commissary line, buying shit and spending money willy-nilly. We must be smart about this and have something to fall back on when we hit the streets. Got it?"

The ladies nodded.

"Good. The clients provided us with a verifiable physical. They are disease free. However, it is imperative that we protect ourselves. We cannot explain away pregnancy. Now that those housekeeping tidbits are handled, here are the assignments for the night."

Assignments contained the clients fictitious name and what service they wanted performed that night. It was up to each woman to make the job interesting to earn extra cash. Electronic tipping was allowed.

Rusty Dinsdale's ranch looked like something from the old Western show, Bonanza, only with twenty-first century, state-of-the-art equipment. He was a multi-millionaire several time over who used to order from Pleasure Palate six out of seven days a week. Business stayed booming with him on the client roster.

When the ladies were dropped off by the barn, it was Rusty who gave them their guided tour. Sure enough, there was a door at the back of the barn that connected to a house his ranch hands used. Not just any old place, this was a four thousand square feet place that any of the ladies would love to call home. He showed Levia, Veronica and Lyric to their rooms.

"Chantal, come with me please." Tonight, Rusty was her client.

She followed him to her room and closed the door.

"Undress slowly," he said, stroking himself.

One-by-one, she unsnapped the buttons on her coveralls, spreading it so her breasts were the focal point. He walked to her and eased the oversized suit down her body then leaned in to lick a nipple. His hand slid inside her panties and touched her pussy. It was soft and hot. Rusty got on his knees. Using his teeth, he took off her panties and crawled between her thighs. Soft kisses covered her flesh before his tongue stroked it.

"Oh, I love it," she sighed.

The feeling of his tongue teasing her flower, was intense. Small shocks sent tingling sensations coursing through her body. He sucked it and gently put his fingers inside. One by one, then three fingers. It was her undoing. Because it had been so long since a man ate her pussy, she came long and hard in his mouth.

"You taste delicious."

Out of nowhere, he handed her a belt-like article and some lubricant. It was a strap-on with an eight-inch dildo.

"Fuck me," he said, before getting on all fours.

She shrugged, lubed his ass, slid in, and went to town. Their skin slapped one another loudly. Chantal squeezed lube in her hand and yanked his penis as she fucked him.

"Oh, wow!" He exclaimed. "Yeah, baby."

Clearly, no one ever thought to do him like that before her.

"Take this dick with your Brokeback Mountain ass."

Ten-minutes later, a powerful orgasm overtook him, and he collapsed on the floor.

Pen Pals

Across the hall, Benji, a local city councilman, sucked on Levia's breasts like he was a nursing child. This was his first time paying for sex. Nervously, he fingered her, but it was too hard and uncomfortable to her.

"Do you like that, honey?" He asked.

"Mmm hmm," she said through a fake smile. "Oh, yes. Keep it right there. I'm cumming," she lied.

He was pleased because he came five minutes ago.

Down the hall, Lance, a pediatrician, made Veronica give him head.

"I love white chicks who suck dick," he said between thrusts.

She sucked his balls and the head of his dick, using her hands to massage his shaft simultaneously. Then, he propped her on all fours. He loved fucking women in the ass. Lance, spread Veronica's butt cheeks wide open and slowly inserted his dick into her small asshole. Halfway in, he began pumping his cock into her butt hole, stretching it

"Ahh," Veronica screamed, yet Lance noticed that she was backing that plump booty of hers up, grinding it against his groin. Clearly, she wanted more meat up her ass, and he was just the man to give it to her.

"Deeper," she said.

He held her by the hips and thrust deeper. Her asshole stretched under the force of his thrusts which were hard and fast. Her ass gripped his manhood hungrily as he plunged into its forbidden depths.

"Un, un, uh," she grunted. "Fuck this ass. Oh, it feels so good to have your big black dick up my tight asshole."

He grinned and continued to fuck her back door, hard. Repeatedly, he slammed his prick up her tight asshole, loving it, plowing it until he could not take it anymore.

"Fuck. Take this shit."

Veronica screamed when she felt hot cum flood her taut hole. Lance could see his liquid leaking out of her gaping hole as he pulled out of her.

"Nice," he said, before collapsing.

Upstairs, Lyric watched herself in a full-length mirror, wind her pussy in a circle, while sitting on Denim's dick. The two of them added up the take for the night. Pen Pals did well, netting over seventy-thousand dollars for one night.

"Who knew people were willing to pay this much for basic sex."

"I did, baby," she moaned.

He gripped her ass and banged until he came in her pussy. She could feel the heat of him coursing through her.

"Fuck," he grunted.

Pressure built up in her stomach. "Oh, Denim." A gush of warm liquid pooled in the small patch of pubic hairs surrounding the base of his dick. It was so runny, he thought she peed on him.

"I love you. This was a great idea," he said.

"I know you do," she said. "Thank you for helping it come to pass."

A couple more rounds for each of them and soon it was time to go. Everything went off without a hitch at the ranch.

"Here you guys go," Officer Rankin, their transporter said, handing each of them cellphones. "Use these to check your account balances and transfer funds only. Do not make calls to your friends and family. When you get off this van, they remain here with me."

He rattled off their log-in information for them, encouraging them to memorize it.

"Woot! Woot!" Levia yelled, seeing her fourteen grand in the bank. She earned a tip tonight.

"Hot damn, I'm in business," Chantal nodded appreciatively. Rusty gave her a five-thousand-dollar bonus for massaging his asshole after she fucked him so good in it.

Veronica smiled but said nothing. She too had earned fifteen-thousand dollars. It was going to get very interesting on the yard for her.

Lyric checked her balance. She had over thirty-thousand dollars in there from tonight. Yeah, she was something like a pimp.

Chapter 10

All of Pen Pal's clientele were rich, but not all of them were famous, so for some, it was easy to give a fake name. That would not be possible for this client. Pastor Bryan Jamal Long of The Refreshing Church was more popular than the hottest rapper and more recognizable than the president. His global ministry was broadcast in twelve countries. The mega-church, located in Birmingham, Alabama had over forty-five thousand members in the main location and over one-hundred thousand combined members in the fourteen satellite churches around the United States. He was handsome, charismatic, sexy, and very controversial. Behind closed doors, he was a freak.

"I take it you know who you are messing with?" He said arrogantly.

"I take it that you don't," she responded.

It seemed obvious to Chantal that he was used to women fawning over him. If he thought that she was about to do that, he had another thing coming. She stared him down and watched as he unfastened his belt buckle. His pants dropped to the floor.

"Hmph," she shrugged.

Pen Pals

He was blessed in more than ways than one. His package was impressive, but then again, so was hers. She turned around slowly and let the black, silk Kimono slide down her body. Then she leaned over and allowed him to check out her fat ass, which swallowed the G-string she wore.

"Just so you know," she began, "This ass was created by God. It is not man-made."

While still bending over, she rolled her ass in a circle and then made the cheeks clap. Unable to resist the temptation, he walked over and grabbed her ass.

"Damn, I've never seen an ass like this before." He drooled.

"Like I said, you don't know who you're messing with. And again, just so you know, I'm going to fuck the shit out of you."

"Yeah, and I'm going to let you."

Chantal turned around and caressed his muscular chest before kneeling in front of him. His manhood stood at attention and jumped when she kissed the tip of it.

"That's a good boy," she said.

She licked her lips and smiled. He stepped closer, placing the tip of his dick on her tongue when she stuck it out for him. Like the pro she was, she took him into her mouth, slowly, making sure it was wet. Her jaws clamped down on him, applying tantalizing pressure.

"Ahh," he exhaled.

She stopped sucking and allowed her tongue to trace the vein on his penis. Up and down, she licked him. Without warning, she grabbed his cheeks and pulled him completely into her mouth. Pastor Long put his hands on her throat and felt his dick print all the way down to her jugular notch.

"Jesus," he said. Knowing that she had swallowed him whole made him harder and hornier. His hips began to pump in appreciation. With every thrust she welcomed him. Her tongue savoring every inch of him.

"Mmm," she hummed. Chantal looked into his eyes and maneuvered her middle finger closer to his anus. She did not ask for permission. None was needed. He was ready for everything that she had for him, so when she slid her finger in his ass, she anticipated that his volcano would erupt soon.

An expert at reading signals, she clamped down even harder and synchronized her head bobbing with her finger movements. His large hands gripped her shoulders to steady him when his knees began to wobble.

"Fuh-ck," he said, voice shaking.

Hot, sweet semen shot down her throat. She backed off his dick and tilted her head so he could stroke it until it was empty, into her mouth. The last little bits of cream, she held in her mouth and opened wide so he could see it before gulping it down.

Normally, she would require a man to eat her pussy before fucking him, but she needed to feel this stallion inside her. While he was still trying to compose himself, she licked the tip of his dick again, making his soldier stand at attention. Out of nowhere a condom appeared in her mouth and he watched in fascination as she rolled it on his dick. She walked to the bed and lay in the center of it. Spreading her legs wide and lifting her knees she pointed to her womanhood. It was glistening with moisture.

"Come here, man of God. Let me take you to heaven on Earth."

He licked his lips, ready to dive-in. Taking his time, he crawled onto the bed and positioned himself between her thighs. While sitting on his haunches, he rubbed the tip of his dick up and down between the folds of her labia. Primed and ready, he slid himself in. His brow lifted, and his nose wrinkled.

"Ahh," she gasped. This was the fattest dick she had ever experienced. He stretched her as he gently eased inside. "Is something wrong?"

"Your pussy is so tight. I had to make sure I was in the right hole." It was so tight he could barely control himself and it took every ounce of restraint not to nut. He was not a minuteman.

Concentrating on her pleasing her, he took his time. Slow, steady strokes were followed by tender kisses on her neck. When he tried to kiss her lips, she turned her head.

"I don't do that."

"You gon' tell me it's too personal like that chick on *Pretty Woman*?"

"Nah, but it brings back bad memories, so I don't do it."

He stopped moving but did not remove himself from her vagina. "Tell me about it."

"Long story short, my step-dad used to come in my room, kiss me and then fuck me. Bad memories."

"Let me take that pain away. God is a healer of all your hurts."

"Are you seriously ministering to me while you're knee deep in my pussy?"

"I don't think God is displeased with me or you for what we are doing."

"I'm getting paid to have sex with you. You're kidding, right?"

"Not at all and the Word says that if a man did not work, he should not eat. Look it up."   Pastor Long's views were partly the reason he was such a controversial preacher. Media outlets and other mainstream preachers had claimed that his congregation was brainwashed. Many bashed him for misinterpreting the Bible. Some claimed that he was a wolf, leading and preying on lost sheep.

"I wanna pray for you and then, I'm going to show you something different."

"Get off me," she asked softly.

He ignored her. Instead, he laid his right hand on her forehead and began to pray for her quietly. He also resumed his stroke. Only this time, it was slower and more intentional. She heard him ask God to heal her mind and her soul. To take all her pain away and erase the bad memories. To help her forgive her abuser and finally, to help her forgive herself. The sincerity in his voice brought tears to her eyes. Her vulnerability touched his soul.

"I got you," he whispered and then kissed her lips gently. This time, she did not turn away.

Their tongues danced around to a sensual beat created by their bodies. He sucked on her bottom lip. Trailed kisses down her neck. And sucked the stiff peaks that formed on her soft globes. Heat permeated from her center and traveled to his loins. A seemingly unquenchable fire roared within him. He could not get enough of her.

"I'll give you a five-thousand-dollar tip if you let me cum in your pussy."

She shook her head. "I'll let you give me a ten-thousand-dollar tip and you can cum in my ass." Fucking him raw should not have been negotiable, but money talked, and bullshit walked.

"Deal." He eased out of her and went for his cellphone on the chair and pecked on the screen rapidly.

Her phone pinged. She went to her bag, grabbed hers and saw that a deposit of ten grand had been deposited into her primary account. Immediately, she transferred it to the savings account she had set-up. Lyric had given her some sage advice about saving and she took notes.

She climbed on the bed, face down, ass up. The pastor removed the condom. It already had some secretions in it. He emptied the contents on his hard dick, using it as lube and then rammed his dick, full force inside the hole.

"Ow," she whimpered. The pain of him entering her all at once was a bit much.

He remained still, allowing her body the chance to get used to him. After a few moments, he began to move slowly. Her pain was replaced with pleasure. He fingered her pussy with two fingers, rubbing her clit with his thumb. This time, the fire consumed them both. Slap, slap, slap, was the noise their skin made when it came in contact. His hips bucked wildly as he strived to go deeper. Her pussy muscles began to involuntarily contract around his dick. Like a blood pressure cuff, it tightened around his hard member.

"I'm cumming," they said in unison.

Pastor Long threw his head back. "Argh," he growled.

She buried her face in the pillow. "Mmm," she moaned into it.

Spent, he collapsed on her backside and she hit the mattress under the weight of him.

"I did not know who I was messing with," he said. "Now I know."

"And knowing is half the battle," she said cockily.

The two showered and dressed. It had been a wonderful night.

On the van, Chantal and the other ladies laughed until they had tears in their eyes.

"And then I said that the reason I did not like being kissed is because my step-father would mess with me after kissing me."

"Step-father? I thought your parents have been married for almost forty years," Veronica said.

All the women rolled their eyes.

"They have. I made it up, Ronnie. It almost threw me off my game when he started praying for me."

"He did what?" Lyric was stunned.

Bit by bit, she gave them the rundown of what happened with Pastor Long, omitting the part about fucking him without a condom. She also did not tell Veronica or Levia that he had given her two tips. That was something only Lyric knew. Before he left, Pastor Long had told her that he wanted to see her weekly. She agreed. Chantal sat back in her seat on the van as they rode back to the compound thinking about the last thing the sexy preacher had said to her.

"You were bought at a price. Therefore, honor God with your body."

Chapter 11

The hole in her pants came in handy. Especially when she went commando. It made for easier access when she wanted the D and right now, she had to have it. She bounced on Denim's dick, while typing on the keyboard at his desk. He held her tiny waist, gyrating beneath her.

"Say it again," he said. "It makes my dick harder."

"Five-hundred-fifteen-thousand-seven-hundred-fifty dollars. That's how much money we have made in forty days."

"Mmm," he groaned. Vigorously he hips pumped. He banged her so hard, her knees hit the underside of his desk. "Shit," he said through gritted teeth.

"Cum for me baby," she said seductively.

Hell, Pen Pals was making almost more money than Pleasure Palate had, and it was only staffed by three women. Knowing that made her wetter. She put her hands on his thighs, leaned her head back into his shoulder and began to grind his dick.

"Right there. Like that."

Lyric groaned as Denim's dick made one last plunge into her hot, slick pocket. The pressure built within her like a swelling ocean as her climax tore through her. Her eyes rolled, her back arched, and her muscles clenched his shaft. Rolling waves of heat coated her pussy. It rolled down to cover her lover's dick and as the sweet, hot nectar flowed thick from her core, Lyric knew she was his. He owned her and with every crashing wave that followed she continued to ride the tide that spontaneously forced his semen to shoot out of him.

The second wave of Lyric's climax brought starbursts before her eyes and she bit her lower lip, bruising the tender flesh. "Oh my God " she cried. Her fingers curled into the papers on his desk and she felt as if she were crashing against the shore. Her body convulsed as she came, until finally her breath caught in her throat and her body stiffened. "Fuck " she mumbled and stilled.

They used baby wipes in his bottom drawer to clean themselves. Denim picked up the papers that had fallen to the floor and wiped the wrinkles out of the pieces that his girlfriend had bunched. He looked at her and smiled.

"I love when your eyes light up like that. You thinking about the good lovin' you just got?"

She giggled, "Of course. I was also thinking that if business kept up, I could recoup my losses in no time."

"I'm still stunned that people are willing to pay so much for sex. How do you do it?"

"Simple, these people equate quality with quantity. The more something is to them, the better it must be. It is really all about knowing your worth and understanding your target consumer. I know wealthy people because I was raised around them my entire life."

Pen Pals

Buzz. The phone on his desk sounded.

"Warden, David Burgen is on line one."

"Thank you, Ellie. Put him through."

"David, how are you?"

"Alive and kicking old man. Is Lyric with you?"

"Yes." Denim pressed the speakerphone button.

They heard him exhale deeply on the other end of the phone line.

"How's it going, young lady?"

"Huh, uh. What is it, David? Somethings up, isn't it?"

"Fatima Scott was found dead in her home today."

"Goody for that bitch. You telling me like I care? She can rest in piss."

Denim cocked his head to the side and hunched in shoulders. He raised his eyebrows, looking quizzically at her, questioning the conversation without speaking. Lyric put her index finger up, indicating she would explain in a moment.

"I know you don't care about her death. It is her life that is interesting. Were you aware that Roman was her nephew?"

"Nephew? How?"

"Fatima was his mother's sister."

Lyric sat down across the desk from Denim, who patiently waited for answers. David went on to explain that he had been investigating her ex-boyfriend since the whole ordeal began. The older gentleman also believed that Lexi and Roman were co-conspirators in some way but wanted to have solid proof before presenting the facts to his client. What he discovered so far was a surprise to him as well.

14

"I'm still working on this. I will call you with updates."

They finished the call after a few more points of discussion. Mind boggling information came her way left and right since she got locked up. If she did not know any better, she would swear someone was trying to take her out...mentally.

"Who is Fatima Scott?" Denim could not wait to ask that question.

"The woman who killed my mom."

Lyric exhaled. Instead of waiting for him to ask, her mind flashed back, and she told him the story that she remembered graphically, as if it had happened yesterday.

Techwood had just gotten locked up. She and her mother, Emma, were living in one of their rent houses. The house that her father was having built for them was not finished yet and the one they were living in prior, was seized by the feds. The rent house and the new build were in a corporation's name not legally owned by her dad, so they could not take it and no one on the streets were aware of the mansion's existence.

"The house we lived in was big, old and needed some upgrades, but it was still beautiful. I used to call it the Money Pit, because it looked much like the house in that movie. One of its issues is that the bathroom door used to jam. The only way to get out was to either leave the door open or pry it open with something. We used a butter knife."

Tears welled up in her eyes. The memory was so fresh. Emma and Fatima were friends. Fatima and her girlfriend, Raylene came over, but she waited in the car. That day, Lyric recalled Fatima's mannerisms.

Pen Pals

"She was antsy. Would not stay still for shit. I did not think anything of it because she said she had to pee. After she used the bathroom, she couldn't get out."

Hot tears streamed down her face as her mind traveled back in time.

"Hold on, the door is stuck. I'm going to get the knife," Emma had said.

Fatima did not hear her say the door was stuck. All she heard was knife and panicked. "My mom stood in front of the door with a butter knife in her hand, preparing to open the door. All I heard was boom, boom, boom. I ran toward the bathroom and saw mommy just as her body hit the ground. There was a bloody butter knife in her hand. Fatima kicked the door open and ran out of the bathroom after shooting my mom and she and her woman took off. David found out that they were planning to rob us that day. Everyone in the hood thought that Techwood had stashed money and dope in the house. They were wrong."

"Why wasn't she locked up for killing your mother? Did she flee the country or something?"

"Nope, she beat the case. Someone paid for her a high dollar attorney who had her plead self-defense. Because my mother died with a knife in her hand, she got off," Lyric hunched her shoulders.

"Man, this is wild. It is pretty evident who paid for the attorney then, since she is related to your ex."

She scratched her head, "yeah, it is all making sense now."

"Do you think that Roman was aware of any of this?"

"Maybe, since most of his family is pretty close. But he would not have fooled with Fatima unless she could do something for him."

"Why do you say that?" Denim asked.

"She was a lesbian. Roman is a homophobe. Hates the very existence of gay people."

"And yet he lives in Atlanta," he scoffed. "Didn't you say his father was your dad's arch enemy?"

"I did and yeah, he is. Casanova, Roman's dad is locked up. Do you think he could have ordered the robbery from inside the joint?"

"It is possible. These bars do not stop business from being handled. Pen Pals is a testament of that."

She paced in his office, rubbing her chin. People who were closest to her were now her enemies. Lexi barely wrote her and had only came to visit twice since she had been locked up. Could she trust anyone? Denim? He was almost too good to be true. Coming aboard Pen Pals so quickly and helping her get money, without question? He did not even ask what was in it for him. Now that she thought about it, he was a little bit too gung-ho for her to start the business.

"Why are you helping me and being so nice? Are you trying to set me up?" Everyone was suspect now.

Denim figured that they would have this conversation one of these days and was prepared for it.

"The only difference between you and I is that you were busted. Long story short, I was raised in the dope game. My family had Larkway Gardens in Birmingham sewed up."

He reached into his desk and pulled out a file, plopping it down on his desk. She walked over and began to riffle through the papers. There was a mug shot and rap sheet for Denver Fletcher.

"Who is this?" She asked, looking up at him.

"My brother. He is at Draper Correctional Center in Elmore, Alabama. A week before I was supposed to leave for college, a rival dealer came to our projects. He shot my brother in the stomach. I shot him in the chest."

"You killed him?" Her eyes grew round. She could not believe what she heard.

"Yes. I thought that he killed my brother. Fortunately for my brother, dude was a poor shot."

"Unfortunately for you, you weren't."

"When the cops arrived, my brother told them that he did it so I could go to school. They took him to the hospital and when he was completely healed, they took him to jail."

"How long did he get?"

"Twenty-years. While I was at school, an official from the Georgia Department of Corrections came and spoke with us regarding lucrative careers with them and the rest is history. I took this job to watch out for my brother. The best way to help him get outside these walls is to be on the inside of these walls. The money I earn with Pen Pals goes straight to an attorney. When I leave this crooked ass job, my brother will be out of this crooked, corrupt ass system."

Lyric was privy to the corruption within the prison system. She had witnessed it firsthand when her dad got locked up. The prison where he was housed was still covering up his murder.

"I understand that. Too bad I did not know you when my dad was alive. Maybe he would not be dead right now. Or at the very least, I would know who killed him."

AVERY GOODE

When Lyric left his office, he pondered what she said. He did have the inside track on a lot of goings on behind the walls. If he made a few calls, he may be able to find the truth about who killed Travis "Techwood" Carter and why.

Chapter 12

evia loved the money she made so far with Pen Pal's and she wanted more. But bigger sacks meant bigger, freakier clients.

"I need a high-roller assignment," she told Lyric.

"Are you sure, Lee Lee?"

"Positively."

Up until that point, she had taken some low-key jobs. Not much sexual activity. A few fetish assignments where she jacked off clients, giving them foot jobs or just getting her pussy eaten. Things like that. Her man would not understand what she was doing and a part of her felt as if she were cheating on him. But Carlos was going to be locked up for another three years and she could not wait for him to get out to make things shake.

"Okay. I will make sure that you get one Friday."

"Yay, thank you," she said.

Her drug possession charge was eligible for sentence commutation. The governor was supposed to be approving thousands of inmate's paperwork and she wanted to be among that number. Robin was doing a great job taking care of her son, but if she got out, Levia was not trying to live with her. Hell, Columbus, Georgia was small and held too many bad memories for her. Nah, she was going to move to Atlanta or one of its suburbs when she got out to make a fresh start.

Friday came quicker than a man fresh out of prison did in tight pussy. True to her word, Lyric made sure Levia had a lucrative client.

"His name is Garrett. He is handsome, wealthy and a generous tipper who likes toys."

Yes, the client was fine. He had smooth, bronzed skin, sexy full lips, and beautiful hazel eyes. The black t-shirt he wore, bulged with muscles. So did his jeans.

"Like what you see?" He laughed at the way she stared at his package and sat down on the edge of the bed.

"Absolutely, Sir."

She kneeled and started to rub her hands and face all over his dick through his Balmain Jeans. When she felt how big and hard it was, she got a little bit intimidated because he was bigger than what she was used to. Nevertheless, she unbuckled his belt, unzipped, and opened his fly and then struggled to pull his dick out of his silk boxers.

"Impressive," she admired.

Once she got it out, she started stroking him for about a minute until something took over her and she indulged herself literally, jamming his big shaft into her mouth. She sucked, bobbing her mouth up and down, licking his shaft and even swirling her tongue around it like a lollipop.

"What is this?" To her surprise he was fully hard and pre-cumming like crazy.

She kept sucking and experimenting with techniques. Twisting, squeezing and gently pulling his wet rod, stimulating him, and turning herself on as well. Before long, she felt his hands on her head. Garrett pushed her down on the floor onto her back, then leaned his pelvic area over her face, forcing her to deep throat his nice, hard dick. A few times she gagged when his dick hit her tonsils.

"That's right. Take this shit," he said before rolling over.

Levia found herself on top of him, dick still in her mouth, salivating over it like a juicy steak. Suddenly, she felt a way like never before. Completely submissive and under his control. Carlos who? Her man was the last person on her mind. While she was on her knees with his manhood down her throat, she felt very dirty, yet more turned on than she had ever been.

Ass in the air, she opened her eyes and looked up at him as he watched her with his joystick in her mouth. It was a look of complete, utter satisfaction. She could tell he liked it and it was obvious, she was pretty much willing to do anything for him. After about thirty minutes, she realized he was purposely not coming.

Seductively she told him, "I want to see you cum."

He started jacking off for her until a huge load of cream blasted up and all over the place. She closed her eyes and let it spray her face.

"My first facial," she admitted, wiping, and licking his juice off. "Yummy."

After a five-minute break, Garrett started touching and rubbing her through her robe before pulling it off.

"Get on the bed."

She did as she was told. As she laid down on her back, Garrett took his pants off. Completely naked now, Levia could fully appreciate all he had to offer. He laid down on his back and beckoned for her to straddle his face. Soon, he was fucking her mouth in the sixty-nine position. Hungrily, his tongue slurped her juice, stroking her box, up and down.

A soft buzz filled the room out of nowhere. Two cold tips touched her. One at her vagina, the other at her anus.

"Relax."

Gently, he eased the double pronged dildo into her. Her asshole puckered, welcoming the painful intrusion.

"Aye," she gasped at the pain of her virginal backside being violated.

Her mouth covered his shaft to suppress a moan of discomfort.

"Shhh," he whispered.

He wrapped his lips around her hardened nub and began sucking on it, still filling her with the plastic dicks. Quickly her pain turned to pleasure, and she was grinding his face.

"Mmm, yes," she said breathily.

The whirr got louder when he increased the vibrating speed. Alternating sucks and thrusts, he brought her to the mountain top. Before she went careening over the edge, he removed it, causing her to feel empty. Garrett sucked on her inner thigh, leaving a hickey at the crease of her thigh. There were beads of sweat that caused their bodies to stick together she noticed when he moved her body off his. She shivered slightly as a breeze from the ceiling fan drifted over her.

"Open wide."

Her legs spread in a perfect V after he produced a flexible string of beads with a ring on the end from his bag. Levia flinched as the plastic toy was rubbed teasingly between her butt cheeks. She was ripe. Her whole body ached with desire. The smell of both of their arousal hung in the air. Garrett's nimble fingers teased her rock-hard nipples before lowering his wandering hand down her flat stomach. Lee Lee moaned loudly as fingers were plunged none too gently between her legs and past her pussy lips. He withdrew, fingers coated in cum that he wiped affectionately on the instrument in his hand.

She tensed as the toy circled her anus. It was in expert hands and soon she had no choice but to relax as the first, large bead penetrated her backside. One by one, the anal beads filled her up. To increase her pleasure, he sucked her clit and fingered her pussy. The teasing continued as she pulled at his shoulders, wanting, needing more than what he offered.

"Fuck me. Please," she begged as heat permeated her core.

"Soon."

Garretts thin mustache was coated in pussy juice. The hairs on his face, tickled her, increasing her arousal as she struggled. Low moans of desire escaped her lips.

"Please," she gasped as her body throbbed with desire.

Unable to hold out any longer with the anal beads still in place, he positioned his Trojan covered dick at the opening of her wetness. In one lunge, he pushed himself hard into her. Skin slapping skin, he drove himself deeper with each thrust. Every stroke, each jab raised their internal temperatures. Pressure built-up. Both had reached their boiling points.

Garrett pulled the beads from her ass and stroked her one last time.

"Yesss," she sang. "I'm cumming." Her orgasm burst through her body, creating a tidal wave of juices, that covered his dick and pooled in his pubic hairs.

One, two, three pumps and his bliss matched hers. Tingling sensations shot through his hard dick.

"Un. Fuck," he groaned. Like a roman candle, his seed shot in spurts inside her until his shaft was empty.

Not long after their breathing returned to normal, they showered together and dressed.

"For your information beautiful queen, Garrett Collier is my real name. When you get out of prison and you are ready for a real man, hit me up." He kissed her on the forehead and left.

Sluts. Thots. Hoes. Tricks. Those were all the names Carlos used to call prostitutes and would call her as well, if he knew what she was doing.

"He can call me whatever he wants as long as he calls me paid in the end."

Ping, her cellphone sounded. A smile spread across her face because of the notification. She happily looked at her account balance and the hefty tip she earned.

"It's beginning to look a lot like Christmas," she sang. But instead of snow, Garrett had made it rain.

Chapter 13

There was something about Veronica that rubbed Lyric the wrong way. She had not done anything directly, but the way she moved around the yard gave the other woman cause for concern. Sometimes she was moody. Other times she was overly cheery. That was not necessarily a bad thing, but it was not typical of the woman she had called friend for the past eight months.

"Have you noticed anything different about Ronnie?" She asked Chantal and Levia as they walked around the track.

"Honestly, I have not paid attention," Levia said. "I have got a lot going on myself."

"I have," Chantal said. "The girl be wilding out on dorm six. She is fucking with a broad over there and they fight all the time. I also heard she's in the hole with Lady Tee."

"The one who be selling drugs?"

"The very one, Levia," she responded.

Lyric shook her head before speaking. "That explains her erratic behavior."

When the three of them rounded the curve, they saw Veronica running across the yard toward them.

"Here she comes," Chantal said.

Droplets of sweat covered Veronica's nose and her high beams were on. Lyric simply stared at her, wondering what she should do. She was not one-hundred percent positive that the woman was on drugs. Rumors like that circulated on the yard about everyone daily.

"Hey guys, what are y'all talking about?" She asked slightly out of breath.

Chantal pointed and twisted her mouth to the side but did not speak.

"Me?" Veronica looked at each of them, but her eyes rested on Lyric who appeared deep in thought.

Am I just being overly suspicious because of what David told me about Roman? The only way to find out the truth was to simply ask, so she did.

"Are you doing drugs, Ron? Word on the yard is that you are in for some big loot to Lady Tee and she is out for blood." She embellished.

Veronica stumbled over her words. "W...wh-ere did you get that from? I, I am not doing drugs."

"So, you don't owe Lady Tee?"

Ronnie shook her head.

"Then why are y'all into it?" Lyric was relentless with her questioning.

"I was messing with this broad on dorm six. She is the one who owes Tee, not me. That is why me and her have been getting into it. I have been fussing at her for messing with that shit when she is so close to going home."

"Dang, girl you had us worried," Chantal said. "You were about to get kicked out."

"For real, Lyric?" Veronica stared at her friend.

"I did not say anything like that, but if you were into that drug shit, then yeah, I would let you go in a heartbeat. You know I love you, but not more than my freedom," she admitted.

It was a brisk December day. Much too cold for Veronica to still be sweating. The wind should have dried the sweat up by now. No, something was not right at all.

"You just gonna kick me out knowing how much I need this money? It's like that?"

She tried to lay a guilt trip on Lyric. The pills she got from Tee were harmless. She just needed something to help her sleep the nights that they did not go out. It was not like she was a junkie. She could stop anytime. In the past, she battled addiction but had been off Smack for seven years before getting locked up. Afterall, it was forgery, not heroin, that landed her in prison.

"No. You are still with us." Outwardly, Lyric smiled. Inside, she cringed.

Was she doing the right thing by allowing Veronica to continue with Pen Pals? She hated second-guessing herself. If recent events had taught her nothing else, it had taught her to trust her gut. They made one more lap around the track before she went to work. Once she was there, she got her cleaning supplies and headed straight to the warden's office. He was out of the office today, but she would see him at the ranch later that night.

She locked the door, plugged up the vacuum and turned it on. Quickly, she logged into his computer and went to their bank website. There were some changes she needed to make. There was no way she was going to get caught slipping twice in her lifetime. If her suspicions were unfounded, she would right her wrongs. Somehow, she knew this time, she was correct. After logging into the site, she made some adjustments then sent an email to David with a few instructions. Five minutes later, she logged off and got busy in the office.

At the ranch that night, Veronica walked in her room. It was dark except for the soft glow of a single candle.

"Undress," the stern voice said.

Obediently she did, then stood naked in front of a masked woman who had a whip in her hand and wore a black leather body suit and spiked six-inch heels.

"Get on the bed," she commanded Veronica.

The sexy nymph got busy with the ropes. Soon Veronica's arms were pulled above her head, tied to the bars of the brass bed. Her naked body was stretched almost painfully, bound securely to the bed posts. One rope was wound tightly above and below her chest, pushing her firm, perky breasts high into the air. The ropes at her ankles secured her legs.

"You seem tense. Swallow this," the woman said.

"Yes, mistress."

The woman gave her two pills and she chased them with a swig of tequila. A gag was placed between her full red lips. She whimpered.

"Silence." The dominatrix whipped her. Red welts formed on her pale thighs.

As promised, she relaxed. The pills made her extremely sensitive and she was turned on by the slightest touch. Her lover gently rolled her tongue around her hard nipple, before taking it into her mouth. She was building an uncontrollable desire in Veronica's body who tried to rub her legs together to create feeling in her pussy, but her bindings prevented it.

"Be still," she demanded, biting Veronica's nipple. The woman kissed and sucked every inch of her lovers' body except where she desired it most.

Ending Veronica's suffering, her lover plunged long, thin fingers into her soaked cunt, rubbing her clit to give her the climax she so desperately needed. Tension mounted within and Veronica's body began to heat up. The client removed her fingers and placed her mouth over the now drenched pussy. Her velvety tongue stroked her walls, lapping up the juices that flowed. She sucked the hard nub, applying just enough pressure to break the dam of passion. Veronica's body spasmed repeatedly until every ounce of cum drained from her body and was swallowed by her lover. Her nipples stood hard and erect and her pussy seeped moisture, leaving it glistening on her bound thighs.

"I need to feel you," the woman said, undressing. She slid one leg underneath Veronica and the other across her, putting them into a scissor position. She used one hand to spread her labia and the other to spread Veronica's until both of their stiff clits, touched one another.

"Mmm," was the only sound Veronica could make when instant shocks ran through her body.

"Oh, yes," her lover sighed with pleasure. The better it began to feel, the harder she grinded her pelvis. Her hips wound wildly as she fucked her lover, creating another fire within Veronica's body, causing another delicious orgasm to overtake them both.

AVERY GOODE

Without saying a word, the woman got up and showered. The loving must have been good the way she stumbled to the bathroom. Spotting the woman's open bag on a chair, Veronica rifled through it and found more pills.

"These things made by pussy pop tonight. I'm sure she won't mind if I help myself to a few more." Quickly, she popped them in her mouth and took a swig of alcohol, swallowing them just as the client exited the steamy bathroom.

"We must do this again. I will be sure to ask for you when I return. Expect a hefty bonus," the client said and exited the room.

Ronnie brushed her teeth to rid her breath of the alcohol smell since that was not allowed, showered, dressed, and headed toward the van. Everyone was present except Lyric.

"It must be too good to stop," Levia said regarding the sex she assumed her friend was having.

It was true that Lyric had made love to Denim, but at present the two discussed her feelings of angst about Veronica and her continuing with Pen Pals.

"Babe do what you feel is best for the organization. I trust you," he said, kissing her deeply.

"The holidays are approaching, and we can make bank. I will probably make my decision afterwards.

Standing on her tip toes, she gave him one final peck and headed to the van. By the time they reached their dorm, they were beat. Veronica felt sluggish. Somehow, she made it to her bunk where she crashed. By noon, she still had not stirred. Her Bunkie came and slapped her hand. It fell off the bed and hung limply.

91

"What the fuck? Bunkie? Bunkie?" She said shaking Veronica. "Somebody help! Call the C.O. Somethings wrong with Ronnie."

A sinking feeling settled in the pit of Lyrics stomach as she ran to the other side of the open dormitory. There she saw Veronica, lying deathly still on her bed. She ran over to her.

"She has a pulse, but it's very weak," she said. "Will one of you bitches please go get some help and stop staring at my mutherfucking friend? Damn!"

The officer on duty ran to see what was happening, followed by a few people on the medical staff. A nurse checked her pulse and looked at her eyelids.

"She's overdosing. Call an ambulance. STAT!"

Lyric backed away from the commotion and turned to face Levia and Chantal. Unbeknownst to either of them, all three women were thinking the same thing. What in the hell did Veronica take and how in the hell was this going to affect Pen Pals?

Chapter 14

cstasy. Marijuana. Cocaine. All the drugs that Veronica tested positive for at the state hospital that the prison rushed her to. The unit manager who assigned her to the overnight work detail was the first to question the supervision of the ladies.

"Obviously, they are not being watched well enough if they can obtain street drugs. We need to launch a full-scale investigation," she said to Officer Rankin, the CO in charge of taking the girls out nightly. He knew what was up, but he played along.

"First of all, Miss Crosby, Inmate Marsh has two failed drug test reports in her file before she was ever placed on this assignment. She's been getting high."

The overweight woman sucked her teeth. Shades of red began at her collar and worked its way to her face. Her breathing became shallow and she clinched her fists.

The officer laughed at her. "Breathe shit, before you blow a gasket. Inmates manage to get clothes, sneakers and even cell phones on this compound, how hard is moving drugs when we don't do cavity searches regularly?"

Pen Pals

The older lady relaxed. "You're right. As soon as Miss Marsh is released from the hospital, she's going straight to the SHU."

"I agree. Let me talk with the warden and see how we need to proceed."

Pacified, she walked off, leaving him to complete the paperwork he was working on. Jay Rankin did not like Peggy Crosby in any way, shape, form, or fashion. Her attitude was almost as bad as her breath that smelled like a thousand pounds of cow shit. The woman did not hide her displeasure when Denim was brought on as warden. Not because he was a young black man, but because she wanted the job. Jay was happy that his homeboy was in the top position. Friends since ninth grade, it was good to work and hustle with him again. When Pen Pal's came about, Jay was glad that his old friend trusted him enough to bring him into an operation of that magnitude. The money was excellent, and he did not have to do anything but transport the girls to and from the ranch and make sure they were safe while they were there. He was not going to allow some broad who looked like the gym teacher in the old Porky's movie and some dopehead to come between him and his money.

The warden was on a call when Officer Rankin got to his office and had whomever he was talking to on speaker phone. He took a seat and did not disturb the conversation that was taking place.

"Emily, what in the fuck did you give Veronica?"

"Just some valium to relax her. She seemed a bit tense."

"That shit was not valium," he seethed, calling her on her lie.

"Fine, it was just a little Ex. Why? What's up?"

"She overdosed, that's what's up. Now everyone is wondering where and how she got them to begin with."

"You have said it yourself that there are more drugs inside the prison than there are on the streets. Just blame it on that."

He gritted his teeth together. "Let me break this down so you understand where I'm coming from. The last time you came to this institution you were a visitor. Next time, you will be a resident."

The resounding threat in his voice got her attention.

"I'm sorry. That was foolish of me. How can I make this right?"

He explained to her in no uncertain terms that a hefty deposit of twenty-five grand would be made no later than five o'clock that evening. Part of it would be a pay-off to Veronica as hush money if needed and the other would be for his inconvenience. As much as he hated to admit it, he did not want to see Pen Pals dissolve. Thanks to Lyric's idea and execution, he and the girls had made more money in a few months than he earned in two years as a warden. It was easy to understand how one got addicted to the lifestyle.

"Crosby wants to launch an investigation," Jay said when Denim placed the phone in its cradle.

"I figured as much. There is no way around it either. If we do not investigate, it will be too suspicious."

"Do we halt business while it's underway?"

"Can't. That will look suspicious, as well. Plus, we have some major clientele coming in for Christmas and New Year's Eve. I'll bury the paperwork until after the holidays and then we'll go from there."

Pen Pals

"Is that wise? Veronica will have to stay in the SHU all that time."

"Get word to her that she will be taken care of and to sleep the time off. She needs to detox if she wishes to continue. She won't be an issue." Officer Rankin forgot to tell her.

A few weeks later, Warden Fletcher ate those words. After learning that the Pen Pals worked the Christmas and New Year holidays, Veronica became salty.

"So, you guys worked without me?"

"Hell, yeah. One monkey doesn't stop no show," Officer Rankin said. His reply set off a hailstorm of vengeance. The more she thought about the money she could have made, the angrier she got. She put in a request of staff, citing that she wanted to confess where she obtained drugs. The case manager was all ears.

"Working on the ranch was a front for a prostitution ring. We would leave here, pretend to work in the barn but really go into a house and turn tricks for shit loads of money with wealthy clients."

The case manager rolled her eyes in disbelief. That is until Veronica got out of her chair, squat, and put her hands down her pants, pulling out a cell phone wrapped in a plastic glove. Appalled at the vulgarity of the gesture but intrigued nonetheless, Miss Crosby called a guard and had her bring her gloves also.

"So, you have a cellphone. That does not prove anything that you just said," she noted, poking the device with a pencil. Even with gloves she did not want to touch it.

"Maybe not, but when I log into my bank account and show you all this money I have and how the corresponding

96

dates of deposit line up with the days and times I was 'at work'," she said, using air quotes, "I bet you'll believe me then."

Miss Crosby saw this as an advantageous scandal. If what the inmate said was true, and she was the one to crack this thing wide open, she would be shoo-in for the warden's job because surely, he would be fired. As much as she wanted to have the young lady retrieve the information right then, there was protocol that must be followed.

"I must get the warden or his assistant to witness this to dispel any rumors of evidence tampering."

"Get whomever you need. I'm telling the truth."

Giddy with excitement, Miss Crosby left out the segregated visiting area and made a beeline to the warden's office.

"Shit, you got some good pussy," he said to Lyric, hitting it from the back as she bent over his desk.

"Uhn, fuck me baby. Make this pussy rain."

The two were going at it like dogs in heat. Over the holidays, Lyric had one of the longest menstrual cycles of her life so she could not get the D, but she did give him head as stress relief.

Miss Crosby walked into the administrative office with the intention of marching straight into the warden's office.

"Just where do you think you're going?" Elnora said, blocking her entry.

"To see Warden Fletcher. It is an emergency. Step aside."

"I'll do no such thing. He is on a conference with Governor Christie. If it were a true emergency, the alarms would have sounded."

"This is important and cannot wait," she insisted, moving quickly around the older woman. "Warden Fletcher, we have an issue," she announced, just has he placed the phone in the cradle.

"What's so urgent for you to barge into my office unannounced?"

She told him of the conversation she had had with Veronica. Denim was flabbergasted that the someone they trusted would sing like a canary. His heart began to beat fast and beads of sweat formed above his brow. Veronica smuggled her cellphone and had tangible evidence against his woman and the other Pen Pals.

"Now do you understand? Let's go."

"I must make a call. Give me five minutes."

Once his door was closed, Lyric crawled from under his desk.

"What the fuck are we going to do? This cannot be happening." He stood and began pacing.

"Oh, but it is," she said. "Just go. Veronica has no clue you are involved. Things will work out. Do not worry about me. I will get to the other ladies and we will get our stories together. Go." She tiptoed and kissed him, sending him into the unknown.

Denim was not sure why she was not nervous like him. She was too cool about it. When he joined Miss Crosby, there were a few other unit team members present.

"Is all this really necessary?" This was getting worse by the minute. But he assumed the reason she called all the others was to show him up. A blind man could see that she coveted his position.

"These are serious allegations. The more witnesses we have, the less room for error."

Denim was not about to let anyone see him sweat. When she started to login into the bank account on her phone, he said a brief prayer. Both Veronica and Miss Crosby sat smugly at the table. Everyone looked on as the website produced an arrow that spun in circles, indicating that it was loading. God heard his prayers. The screen said "Oops. It looks like some data is not loading. Some things may be missing on the page below. Try again in a few minutes."

"Really, Crosby? You brought us all down here for a lie?" Another unit manager asked.

She looked harshly at Veronica.

"I'm not lying," she protested. "It may be the cellphone. If I had a computer, I could show you."

They brought over a laptop. Same thing.

"If she really has an account, call the bank. It's still early," someone joked. They were thoroughly amused at their discomfort. However, the inmate was serious and pulled out her phone and placed the call.

Veronica followed the prompts on the call. She put in her social security number as instructed.

"We're sorry, there is not an account associated with that number. Please reenter or press zero to speak to a representative."

Frustrated, she opted to speak to a human. The representative came online and was just as useless as the automated system. There was no record of an account holder named Veronica Marsh at Georgia National Bank.

"Ahh!" She screamed. "I have over eighty-thousand dollars in that bank. Look at my phone, I screenshot my account information. It shows my name, balance and all that."

Pacifying her, Warden Fletcher put on a pair of gloves, powered on the device, and went to the gallery. It was empty. The entire phone was. Veronica went ballistic and jumped up, trying to swing on her case manager.

"You stole my money, bitch!" She accused before being carted off, back to her cell in the segregated housing unit, or the SHU as the inmates called it. All the staff stared at Miss Crosby with disdain, who hung her head in embarrassment, before walking out the room.

"We can forego the investigation," she said. "I was wrong."

The next day, when Lyric came to clean his office, he picked her up and kissed her.

"You are a bad ass, Miss Carter. No wonder you were not worried. It was already handled. What did you do?"

"I had Jay pull her file a few days before she went out that last time. I knew she was doing drugs then. That day you were out of the office. I logged onto the bank site and transferred the money to our primary account, before dividing it amongst Lee Lee, Chantal, and Jay. Then I emailed David and had him call our bank rep who deleted any records of her having an account. After that, he called my connect at the cellphone company and he did a hard reset on her phone, which deleted all pics, contacts, everything. Something told me she was going to sing like a canary. This time, I am glad I followed my hunch."

Hindsight was a bitch. She was not going to make the same mistake twice.

Chapter 15

One greased palm. Two favors. Three phone calls. That is all it took for Denim to find out who killed Techwood. Now, he sat in his office, waiting for David to arrive, so they both could give Lyric the information that each of them discovered. He knew her well enough to know that she was going to be devastated.

"This is fuckery," he whispered while reading the notes in the file.

The phone on his desk buzzed.

"Mister Burgen is here, Sir."

"Show him in, please."

His secretary gladly stood to show the handsome man in.

"This way," she said with a flourish of her hand. He walked ahead of her toward the office. She may be older, but she was still young enough to appreciate the man's firm backside.

"Close the door on your way out," Denim said with finality.

They briefed one another on their findings. The phone buzzed again. This time, it was Lyric. The first person she saw was Denim. She greeted both men and stopped in her tracks, feeling uneasy as the two men remained quiet.

She stared into her man's eyes. There was no light in them, and they were slightly downcast. His shoulders too, were slumped.

"Take a seat," he said gravely.

"I don't like the sound of your voice nor the look on either of your faces. What's up?"

"Well, after I did a little digging, I found out some things that you may not like. We both did."

"Such as?"

"For starters, Roman knew who you were all along when the two of you first met. His father is Leonard Traylor, known on the streets as Casanova."

"Wait, what? His name is Roman Jones." Realization dawned on her. "Is Jones his mother's last name?"

Denim nodded and exhaled before continuing. "Casanova is the one responsible for your dad's death. He ordered the hit on him in the chow hall that day."

Tears burned her face as they poured. "How did you find all this out?"

"Me and David had our suspicions but I'm a warden. I have done a few favors for some inmates here and there. Called in a few markers."

When she remained silent, he sat in the chair next to her, scooted closer and rubbed the small of her back. Slowly, she leaned her head on his shoulder and cried. For her father and for herself. No, she was not feeling sorry for herself, but she was angry for wasting her time and energy caring for someone like her ex-boyfriend.

"Roman worked with his father to ruin your family. Casanova blamed Techwood for getting busted. He believed your dad set him up, so he retaliated. He thought that you all would lose everything like he did, after Techwood was locked up, but that didn't happen," he added.

"He didn't have someone like you, David," she said, wiping her eyes.

"Nothing he tried worked. Not even the attempted robbery that kil-..." Denim's voice trailed off.

"Killed my mother," she finished for him softly. "Damn. He killed both my parent's."

Everything that the men found out was going to be a bitter pill to swallow. There was no way to soften the blow, so David picked up where Denim left off.

David began. "Um, the reason why Alexis stopped coming to see you is because she was pregnant."

Lyrics head dropped, chin hit her chest and mouth flew open. David pursed his lips, waiting for the inevitable question.

"By who? The married man she was fucking with before I got locked up?"

"Uh, she wasn't messing with a married man. Not at that time anyway. She was sleeping with Roman. That's who fathered her child."

She jumped up so fast her chair tilted backwards. "Sonofabitch! I knew something wasn't right with them, but I just couldn't put my finger on it." Slowly, she sat back down. "Was pregnant? She had the baby?"

"Yes, in November. A little girl named, Romani Pierra Jones."

"What in the ghetto baby name bullshit is that? Really?"

Denim shook his head at the name. David giggled and continued providing her with the information he discovered. Everyone who worked to get Lyric convicted was all a part of Roman and Alexis's scheme. The cops who arrived first on the scene, the judge, prosecutors, everyone. It was a well-orchestrated set-up.

"I wondered how your case moved through the system so quickly," David said. "Most cases like this sit on a docket for at least a year after arraignment. I should have known something was awry."

Before continuing, David leaned over, reached into his briefcase, and pulled out an envelope. Inside there were copies of documents that Roman had filed with the state courts, assigning ownership of Carter Holdings to Amber Williams.

"I'm confused, I thought that Alexis had ownership."

"She did at first, Lyric. But like you, she was tricked into signing."

"Where is she now? I haven't gotten a letter from her or heard anything about her lately."

"She's a woman scorned. Roman left her broke and alone with their daughter. He got married."

"Married? To whom?" She was astounded.

"Amber."

Exhaling, David laid it all out. From the beginning, Roman played both Lyric and Lexi. He and his father constructed a plan to get the Carter's money, but it was not until Amber came along that he found a way to seal the deal.

Instantly, he was attracted to her and began a sexual relationship with her almost immediately. Because she was a minor, he used that to his advantage. It was he who encouraged her to join Pleasure Palate and convinced Alexis to lie about the young girls age. That is how the pandering under-age participants charge came about. He used Alexis to secure the assets initially and then had them transferred to Amber, who he always wanted to marry. As her husband, he could control all her interests.

"Something told me to dig deeper, so I did. I found an address for Tammy Williams, Amber's mother and went to visit her in Alabama." He pulled out some pictures and showed them to Lyric and Denim, one by one.

Tammy was a beautiful woman who appeared to be mixed. With long, strawberry blond hair, and green eyes, it was easy to see where Amber got her looks from. The next picture was a mug shot. The woman was disheveled. Her face was drawn, and her eyes were sunk in.

"These pictures are the mother, before and after drugs. The mugshot was taken two weeks ago. When I found her, she was in jail. For her cooperation, I bailed her out and agreed to give her some money. Currently, she is at an in-patient rehab center. She wants to be a better mother to her daughter, Amber."

"Why now? Her daughter is good as grown now that she's married," Lyric said.

"I said that, also. Check this out, though." He handed her a photo of a beautiful girl, who was a much younger version of Tammy, in a cheerleader uniform.

"Who the fuck is this?" Lyric gave the picture back to David.

"That is the *real* Amber Williams."

Pen Pals

"Bullshit," she said. "It resembles her but that is not the woman who works for me."

"Yeah, I know. This is not who worked for you, but trust me, that is Amber. _This_ is who worked for you."

David gave her a third picture.

"Wowww," Denim said.

"You have got to be kidding me."

The same beautiful strawberry blond hair. The same beautiful green eyes. Tammy's children could have passed for twins.

"Meet Aida Williams, transsexual, formerly known as Aidan. He began his transition when he was twenty-one. At the time of employ at Pleasure Palate, he was twenty-five. His mother said prostitution covered the cost of his surgery which was well over one-hundred grand."

It hit Lyric like a ton of bricks. Roman was married to a man. Palm to face, all she could do was sit in silence for a while. Then out of nowhere, the laughter began.

"Ha, ha, hee, hee," she said, doubled over. Tears streamed down her face, but this time, they were happy ones. "Fair exchange ain't robbery."

"We need to start working on your appeal. This information will help you win. My brother will take the case." The shrewd businessman got up to leave. "One more thing. No offense," he said to the warden. "Do you have any footage of you having sex with Mister Jones?"

She did and told him where to find it. The time was past for being bashful. Her freedom was at stake.

"Thanks, his unethical and unscrupulous behavior will help him get disbarred."

David left shortly after that. Leaving Lyric to sort out all the information he just dumped in her lap.

"Can you believe that?" She asked Denim after David left.

"At first I couldn't. It seemed like a page out of a fiction book, but it's real."

"Right. I wonder what David has up his sleeve?" She said.

Back in his office, David called Roman and set up a meeting with him and his wife. He was about to stack the deck in Lyric's favor.

Chapter 16

ut the key players in place. Create a sticky situation and watch as the drama unfolds. This is what makes reality television so good. David was aware of this. So, like a good producer, he did that. Roman and his wife were right on time. They were sitting in the waiting room when Tammy Williams came into the office. From the monitor on his desk, David watched it all play out.

"What are you doing here?" Tammy asked her child.

"I was about to ask you the same thing."

"Who is this?" Roman asked. The woman was fine as hell.

"Um, let's go babe. She's not important."

"Is that any way to treat your mother?"

"Your mom? Hey, it is a pleasure to meet you. Amber has told me so much about you."

"No, I have not," a young girl said, who had just entered the room.

Roman felt a tug at his arm. "Please, babe. Let's go," his wife pleaded, but he yanked his arm away.

"Who are you?" Roman's eyes squinted, and his breathing pattern changed. Something fishy was going down and whatever it was, his wife did not want them to be there, which made him want to stay even more.

"I'm Amber. Amber Williams. Nice to meet you. Where have you been big head? I have missed you," she teased playfully.

"Wait, your name is Amber, too? How is it that your mom has two children named Amber?"

"You are so daft," the teenager said to Roman, giggling.

"I don't," she said. "This is Amber," she pointed at her teenaged daughter. "And this is," she paused. Her son's eyes pleaded with her not to go any further, but she did not take heed. "my son, Aidan. He's a transsexual."

"You're a fucking man?" Roman yelled.

"Well actually, you're fucking a man," the real Amber teased.

Her comment was like waving a red flag to a bull and in the same manner, Roman charged at his partner, in a bitter rage. Aidan, who tried to run away, tripped over the edge of the coffee table, falling onto the floor. Swiftly, Roman wrapped his hands around the slender neck and tried to squeeze every ounce of life out of him.

"I'm going to kill you," he yelled furiously.

Shaking his head, David watched the melee unfold. He picked up the phone and dialed security, asking that they come immediately and to also phone the police. If they did not come soon, someone was going to die. Although Tammy and her son, had an estranged relationship, she did not want to see any harm come to him. To save he baby boy, she jumped on Roman's back and began pounding his shoulders. He shook her off like a rag doll.

Aidan thrashed around violently to get Roman off him to no avail. His mother and sister did all they could to help him, but the angry man held on with bulldog tenacity. By the time security arrived, he had lost consciousness. Amber and Tammy wailed as one security guard performed CPR, while another detained Roman. The police and paramedics arrived at the same time. Prepared, David came out of his office, video tape and briefcase in hand. In less than twenty minutes, the outcome he predicted came to pass. He counted on Roman's homophobia to get the best of him.

A cop arrested Roman for attempted murder and read him his rights. "With these rights in mind, do you wish to speak to me?"

"Kiss my ass, pig," he spit on the officers' badge.

"Guess that's a no. Take him away."

"Here's the footage of the fight. My office has camera's. Unfortunately, the sound is broken," David lied.

"Sonofabitch. You set me up. I promise I'm going to kill you for this."

"Not a smart thing to say in front of the police," David laughed. He turned to Tammy when the paramedics raised the gurney to take Aidan away. "Go with your child to ensure he's…I mean she's okay. We can conclude our business later. Your baby is most important."

She hugged him, and they left. David gave his waiting area the once over. The night janitors would clean up the mess. Because he figured there would be some level of violence, he gave his secretary the rest of the day off. No sense in putting her in danger.

He locked up his office and walked to the other end of the hallway where his brother's law practice was. Seth

Burgen was one of nation's preeminent defense attorneys. Had he been in the country when Lyric was first arrested, he would have taken her case, and all this could have been avoided. But everything happens for a reason. All the snakes surrounding Lyric were weeded out and despite the circumstances, she met a guy in which David approved.

Seth filed documents in court citing ineffective counsel with claims that Roman required sex as a condition for legal defense for Lyric. He also presented evidence that resulted in an investigation against all parties involved in the case of the Midtown Madam, as the local news reports began calling her.

A judge, who was a close friend of Seth's signed off on the motion for the court to vacate the sentence of Lyric Elaine Carter. Considering the corruption case, the prosecution did not object. Twenty-four hours later, David drove to the prison for the last time. This time when he left, he was taking his best friends' little girl with him. She was a free woman.

Chapter 17

Leonard "Casanova" Traylor had talked a lot of shit on the yard, bragging about his son the high-powered attorney and how much money he made. Roman's connections granted his father preferential treatment in the prison. Casanova walked around with bravado, almost as if he were untouchable, treating some inmates any type of way. In doing so, he created many secret enemies.

The day his son's case was aired on the news, the entire C block where he was housed, was watching. Everyone knew that his son got convicted and disbarred and there was nothing he could do or say. He knew that he was hated by many. Most bosses were. The issue was, he really did not know who his enemies were because everybody was down with you while you were up, especially in the joint.

Now that Roman was prison bound, the armor Casanova once had was no longer available, so he treads lightly. He stayed in his cell more than he used to and he only hung around guys he was certain he could trust. It was one of those guys who came to him and told him the worst news possible.

His son was down in intake and would be housed on the same unit as him.

With his head hung low, Casanova closed his eyes and prayed. He regretted involving his son in his revenge plot against Techwood. Even in death, his rivalry still won. Now, because of him, they would both live the rest of their lives behind bars.

It took a few hours for Roman to make it to the unit. By the time he arrived it was lockdown. On the way to his cell, he stopped when he saw his father's face in the small plexiglass window.

"I'm sorry I let you down, Pops," Roman said with tears in his eyes.

"Nah, Son. You have made me proud. Believe that," he admitted.

"Move along, Jones," the CO said.

"We will talk in the morning on the way to chow. I have another plan," Casanova said.

Roman got to his six by eight-foot cell and climbed on the top bunk. All he could do was stare at the ceiling. Regardless what his father said, he had let him down. He let himself down. Somehow, sleep overtook him, and he rested. The next morning, after washing his face and brushing his teeth, he went to his dad's cell.

"Son don't worry about anything. I have a plan. Come, let us go eat breakfast. They are serving my favorite, grits, and bacon. While we eat, I'll tell you what I got up next."

"Sure thing, Pops." Roman hugged his father tight, hesitant to let him go, but he did.

They talked casually on their way to the chow hall. The line was long. Three inmates in front of them began to argue.

It was unclear over what. Someone cursed. Another threw a punch. The fight was on. A sense of Déjà vu washed over Casanova. The scene was all too familiar. He grabbed his son and moved away from the tussle. But he did not move quickly enough. In quick succession, someone stabbed him three times from behind. He was still holding Romans shirt when he went down. Thud, Roman heard before turning around.

"Pops!" He screamed in anguish, dropping to the ground to hold his dad.

Warm blood seeped through his fingers as he tried to apply pressure to the wound.

"Hold on, old man. I got you. Somebody get some help," he pleaded.

Inmates milled around like nothing out of the ordinary was going on. Some even continued through the chow line, until the guards on duty finally arrived. One kneeled next to him and said, "Well, well, well, Traylor. You finally got your comeuppance," he said quietly before radioing for more help.

Roman did not hear what the man said. He cried loudly.

"Don't die on me, Pops. Please. I need you man. I love you."

"I love you too, Son. I. Am. Proud. Of. You."

Casanova looked up. It was then he remembered why all this seemed so familiar. This is the way Techwood died, after he ordered the hit. He looked at his son and then thought about Lyric. His son would be fatherless just like she was. Before he closed his eyes for perhaps the last time, Casanova thought that fair exchange ain't no robbery.

AVERY GOODE

✏️

The view from the overwater bungalow in Bora Bora was breathtaking. Six months ago, Lyric could only dream about being here but today, it was her reality. She looked over at Denim and smiled. He was everything that she needed plus a whole lot more. Had her father been alive, he would have liked him.

"Hey, you," he said as he walked up behind her, leaned over and kissed her on the neck.

"Hey, babe," she said, leaning back into his arms.

Turned on, he nuzzled her neck. Something quickened in her woman parts. The white foam of the Pacific Ocean rolled in and splashed on the deck, but it was not the water that made her wet. She rubbed her ass against the bulge in his swim trunks.

"Now," she said with urgency, straining to pull his member through the hole.

Without hesitation he leaned her over the railing, moved her bikini bottoms to the side and positioned the head of his rod at her wet opening. As much as he wanted to ram himself fully inside her, he exercised great restraint. Using slow, steady strokes, he glided back and forth. She reached around him, grabbing his thigh, and tried to take more of him within.

"Stop playing and fuck me." Desire and need filled her voice.

Denim grabbed the sides of her small waist and thrust forward.

"Ohh," he moaned. She felt so good, so tight, wrapped around him.

Skin slapped skin. The sun beamed down on them, tiny beads of perspiration cascaded down his chest, landing on her ass cheeks. Pressure built up within them. An insatiable need lingered between them. The more he stroked the greater the pressure. He could not get enough of her. She could not get enough of him.

"Baby," she purred. "Right there. Keep it there."

The force of his thrusts increased. His dick swelled inside her. Lyrics back arched as a powerful orgasm overtook her, making her wet pussy rain with nectar. Denim's knees locked as he came, filling her with hot semen.

They fixed their bathing suits and sat on the chaise lounges.

"I love you, Misses Fletcher."

"And I love you, Mister Fletcher."

He held her hand and caressed it with his. There was a light in his eyes when he looked at his new bride.

"For a few months, after you were released, I would sit in my office and stare at the door, expecting you to bust in without knocking, like you used to do."

That made her laugh. "Yeah, I was kinda rude. Who did they get to replace me?"

"Ms. Oshima. She was very thorough. Never gave me any lip about taking out the trash either, like some people I know, but I am not saying any names."

"Whatever. I bet she did not give you any head, like some people you know either." She playfully punched his arm.

"None of that. But she did look all sexy in her gray uniform, with her oxygen tank in tow."

"I never understood that. Doctors put her on oxygen because smoking is ruining her lungs and yet, she still smokes. When she would come sit outside and I would see her lighting a cigarette, I would run the other way. Ain't no way I'm going to sit around and blow up with your dumb ass."

They both laughed.

"Things were not the same on the yard after you left. I felt it and so did the other inmates. Regardless of the situation or where you were, you brought something special to that place. It was hard for me to be there."

"Aww, hubby wubby, missed me."

"Damned straight I did."

Things changed further when Levia's sentence was commuted and she and Chantal were released. Shortly after, Jay quit. Enough was enough. It was not until his brother was released though, that Denim resigned as warden. Everyone he loved was now out of prison and his work inside the walls was over.

As soon as he got to Atlanta, he called his woman who welcomed him into her home. She texted him the address and made a beeline to her house. When she was still incarcerated, she would come to his office and they spoke for hours about her life on the outside. The house that her father had built was one of them. In her description, she would tell him how beautiful it was but when he first saw it, her words did it no justice. She told him it was big, but he was not expecting a mansion. It was there he proposed. His eyes lit up at the memory and his mouth curled slightly at the corners.

"What are you over there smiling about?" She asked.

"A couple of things. The first time, I came to see you at home and the day I proposed to you."

"That was the same day, babe."

"I know. When the door swung open and I saw your face, I knew then that I did not want to be apart from you one second longer."

"Man, I did not know what you were doing when you got down on your knee. I was like, get up and come inside but you were like, no, this is something that cannot wait."

That day, he was a bundle of nerves because although he and Lyric had continued their relationship outside the prison walls, he was not sure if her feelings were still as strong.

"Babe, I was so nervous to ask you because I did not know if your feelings were the same. In prison, everything is intense because you are confined, and the options are few. But you were free, and the world was your oyster. Thank you for saying yes."

"Thank you for asking me. My love for you is genuine. The only thing prison did was it allowed me to see who you really were. You went hard for me there and put so much on the line for me. I will never forget that."

Denim swung his legs over the side of the chaise lounge and laughed. "You said you were broke but still had the house your dad built. Imagine my surprise when I first saw it. Outside it was enormous, but inside? Damn, that house was straight palatial."

"*Our* house, and I never said I was broke. You said that. I said I needed to recoup my loss after Roman and Lexi stole my stuff."

He chuckled. "That's one of the reasons I let you start Pen Pals. I felt bad for you and thought I was helping you."

"You were. You helped all of us."

"Too bad I could not help Veronica."

"You tried. None of us knew how bad her issues were. Turns out, she lied about her sister losing her job and the house. She did not have any sisters."

Veronica was released from the hole three weeks after Lyric left. She copped some more drugs from Lady Tee and overdosed again. This time, there was no saving her and she died. In retrospect, Lyric often wondered if there were signs that she missed. After all, she was blindsided by her former friend and ex's deception.

As if he picked up on her thoughts, he asked, "do you miss Alexis?"

"Sometimes. She was more than my best friend. We were raised as sisters. The last time we spoke, I told her I forgave her, but it would take some time deal with her again."

"What about ol' boy?"

"I don't miss him. And if I am honest, I never loved him either. He was comfortable and we worked well together, but there was always something missing. Now I understand what that was. It was love. When he first betrayed me though, all I wanted was revenge."

"Now what do you want?"

"You. Vengeance is mine said the Lord. He will take care of Roman and his father."

"God is truly on their side. Casanova should be dead right now instead of paraplegic."

"Enough of that. I am in Bora Bora with the man of my dreams. My sister, Chantal, just married Garrett, the man of hers. Levia is happy with Jay and her children and no one else matters."

Lyric moved from her chaise and went and cuddled with her husband. The least of her worries were Roman, his murderous father or Alexis. That was her past, this was her future.